"Don't," She Started to S...
but I...

Sarah felt her ...
lightly caressed ...
mouth. Her kn... ...ly and her
hands stopped trying to push him away. . . .

He lifted his lips for a moment. "That's better," he muttered.

Sarah opened her eyes. His face was unreadable except for the desire Sarah saw there. As she watched his mouth move closer and closer, she began to feel heat coursing through her body. This time when his lips touched hers, they parted willingly. . . .

THEA LOVAN

was a history major in college and always had a consuming interest in faraway people and places. She works now as a travel writer and has visited some of the most exotic corners of the world.

THEA LOVAN
A Tender Passion

Silhouette Romance

Published by Silhouette Books New York

America's Publisher of Contemporary Romance

Silhouette Books by Thea Lovan

Passionate Journey (DES #28)
A Tender Passion (ROM #281)

SILHOUETTE BOOKS, a Division of Simon & Schuster, Inc.
1230 Avenue of the Americas, New York, N.Y. 10020

ISBN: 0-671-57281-4

First Silhouette Books printing March, 1984

10 9 8 7 6 5 4 3 2 1

Map by Ray Lundgren

America's Publisher of Contemporary Romance

Printed in the U.S.A.

A Tender Passion

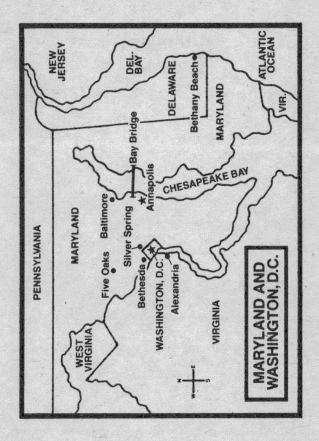

MARYLAND AND
WASHINGTON, D.C.

Chapter One

Sarah Bennet leaned back on the hard wooden bench hidden in a corner of Rock Creek Park and let the weak rays of the spring sun warm her. She looked around absently without really seeing the new green of the budding trees or the brightly colored tulips swaying in the breeze.

It was early morning and, except for an occasional jogger, Sarah had this part of the park completely to herself. However, it was not the pure morning air, the beauty of the flowers or the solitude of the park which had brought her out so early.

Instead, a restlessness new to Sarah had driven her out of her tall, narrow house in Georgetown and into the park as the sun had come up. At first she had tried walking briskly, but that hadn't helped to alleviate her discontent. Sarah felt dissatisfied and she was aware of a strange longing in her body.

Dissatisfied with what? she asked silently. Surely she wasn't dissatisfied with her life. Not now, not after all

7

the time and effort she had put into her business. The
hard work and frustration had paid off. Success was
finally coming her way. No, there was no reason to be
dissatisfied on that score. The lean years were over and
her career as a fashion designer had taken off. She
wasn't a world-famous designer by any means, but she
did count some of the best-dressed women in Washington, D.C., as her clients. And in the front of her home
in Georgetown, she had a small boutique where she
displayed and sold the designs she created.

But if it wasn't her career, then what was causing this
edginess which had pushed her into the pale, early
morning sunshine? Was it her love life . . . was that
what was depressing her?

Sarah considered her love life carefully. Bill Baker,
the man she had been dating for the past six months
was nice enough but . . . face it, she told herself with a
sigh. He isn't anything to write home about. But that
wasn't the point. Bill was the point. Bill and their
weekend dates. Every Friday and every Saturday evening, for the past six months, they had gone to dinner, a
movie or a concert. Every weekend their dates were
predictable, correct . . . and boring.

Sarah had drifted into this arrangement partly because she hadn't wanted to hurt Bill, who seemed
genuinely fond of her, and partly because their evenings out were a pleasant change from the work-filled
routine of her life. But now, she felt she wanted
more—more excitement, more glamour. Bill could
provide neither, and it was unfair of her to expect it
from him. He was nice, and he'd make some lucky
woman a good husband, but he was not an exciting
man.

Sarah sighed. Nice or not, he was also dull. And all
of a sudden, Sarah no longer wanted dull evenings in a
concert hall. She wanted gaiety, spontaneity, long
lingering glances over wine-filled glasses, cheek to
cheek, heart to heart dancing to slow soulful music.

Something was missing from her life, she told herself unhappily. Once she had thought she would be the happiest person alive if only her career would take off. Obviously she had been wrong. She wanted, needed something else in her life. But what?

For a moment, a noise somewhere off to her right broke into Sarah's thoughts. She looked around her, but there was no one nearby. She seemed to be alone in her part of the park. She cocked her head and listened intently, but she heard nothing more. It could have been a cat, she told herself, or even the wind sighing in the trees.

Her thoughts returned to Bill and the sameness of their dates. For the first time, she was aware of the lack of some vital spark in their relationship. Though she had been seeing him for nearly six months now, their relationship was still platonic. Bill kissed her good night after each date, but on the occasions his kisses had threatened to prolong themselves or get out of hand, Sarah had immediately removed herself from his embrace. Early on in their relationship, Sarah had made it clear to Bill that sexual involvement was out of the question. She had neither the time nor the inclination. Men had always played second fiddle to her passion for designing beautiful clothes. He had accepted her edict in the same calm manner with which he accepted everything.

Then she had been glad. Now his lack of ardor infuriated her. Wasn't she attractive enough to be pursued ardently? Wasn't she the type of woman to inspire passion? Sarah's thoughts broke off with a kind of shocked surprise as she realized where they were taking her.

Do I want to be swept off my feet? she asked herself incredulously. To be wooed with flowers and poetry, to be won with fiery kisses and promises of love? Was the tall, dark stranger, famous in fiction, what she was secretly wishing for?

It didn't seem possible. Could it be that she—cool, purposeful Sarah Bennet—was feeling restless and dissatisfied because there was no romance, no passion in her life?

No, Sarah told herself uncomfortably. It couldn't be that. If Bill had forced the issue, if he had rained passionate kisses on her lips and face, she would have refused to see him again. That she knew for a certainty. But what, then, was the problem?

Once again the sounds of choked-off sobbing interrupted her thoughts. This time she caught enough of the noise to know it was not caused by a mewing cat or the breeze rustling through the trees. Sarah got to her feet. There was something to the sound which she could ignore no longer. She had to find out where it was coming from.

Quietly, she followed what now sounded like muffled sobs. As she traced the crying to a thicket of shrubs, the sobs grew more intense. Her heart beating quickly, Sarah walked over to the shrubs. She was too tenderhearted to ignore the misery of another person. She pushed aside some of the shrubs, and what she saw there tore at her heart.

There, curled up in a ball on the ground was a child, with a puffy face stained by tears and dirt. The girl was dressed in a green skirt and white blouse with some kind of insignia on the pocket. A school uniform, Sarah surmised. She dropped to her knees and managed to resist an almost overwhelming urge to take the crying girl in her arms. She was surprised by the intensity of her feelings, but there was something about this child which reminded her of herself. It wasn't her appearance, for the little girl was fair whereas Sarah was dark. Perhaps it was the way the child was curled up on the ground as if her misery were too great to bear.

"Don't be afraid," Sarah said gently as the little girl started. "I heard a noise and I came to investigate."

"I didn't think anyone was around." The little girl's

voice quivered as she spoke. "It was so quiet. I thought I was alone."

The girl looked at Sarah suspiciously. "How long have you been here in the park?" Her crying had stopped, but she was shivering in the cool morning air.

Sarah looked down at her watch. "Almost an hour," she said in surprise. "I had no idea it's been that long. I was thinking about . . . it doesn't matter what I was thinking about," she finished a little lamely. She slipped off her delicate, hand-knit sweater and wrapped it around the girl's shivering shoulders.

"You look as though you slept here," Sarah remarked as she brushed away some twigs and brown, dried leaves from the girl's skirt and blouse. Now that she had discovered the little girl, she had no idea what to do next. The girl, who appeared to be about ten, was physically unhurt and Sarah didn't know whether she should pry into whatever it was that was hurting her emotionally.

"I did," the girl said.

"Did what?" Sarah asked, startled. Perhaps she had missed something.

"I slept here," the girl said defiantly.

Sarah sat back on her heels and looked at the girl in consternation. Visions of the girl, cold and vulnerable through the dark night, crowded into her mind. Safe though it was considered to be in the daytime, Rock Creek Park was no place for a girl, especially a young girl, to spend the night. Sarah was horrified.

"No wonder you're cold," she said finally, trying not to let her shocked surprise show. "What's your name?"

The girl gave Sarah a careful look. "Ginny," she said finally.

"Ginny? Ginny what?"

"Just Ginny," the girl said firmly. It was obvious she didn't want to talk about herself.

Sarah did not press her. "I'm Sarah Bennet," she said instead. "I don't live too far from here. Why don't you come home with me? You can have a hot bath and some breakfast. After that perhaps you can tell me why you spent the night in the park."

Ginny regarded her suspiciously. "Are you going to call the police?"

"I don't think so," Sarah replied calmly though her heart was beating quickly. What would she do if the little girl refused to come with her? "You don't look like the wanted, criminal type to me."

That got a giggle from the girl. To Sarah's relief, she climbed stiffly to her feet. In good conscience, Sarah couldn't have left her there, but she couldn't have dragged her kicking and screaming through the park either.

After a hot bath, Ginny sat in the small kitchen of Sarah's house devouring a plate of scrambled eggs. She was wrapped in a warm, fluffy bathrobe of Sarah's. Though Sarah was petite, the bathrobe seemed to wrap around Ginny twice, and the sleeves would have fallen into her eggs if Ginny didn't keep pushing them back.

The sight of the little girl struggling to eat her breakfast brought a smile to Sarah's face. She sat across the table from Ginny sipping a glass of orange juice and wondering how in the world to proceed.

"Now, perhaps you'd like to tell me what you were doing in the park all night," Sarah said when the eggs were almost gone.

Ginny took a big sip of orange juice. "I ran away," she said. Her defiance had returned.

"I guessed that much," Sarah said dryly. "What I want you to tell me is why you ran away. Was it something your parents did?"

Tears filled Ginny's eyes and her defiance was momentarily replaced by unhappiness. "I don't have any parents. They died in a car crash a few months ago."

Sarah was beginning to understand her strange identification with this child. "How old are you, Ginny?" she asked gently.

"Ten."

That explained it. Sarah, too, had lost both her parents when she was ten. No wonder the unhappiness of this girl pulled at her heartstrings. Sarah knew far too well just how she felt.

"I'm sorry about your parents," she said slowly. Memories swept over her. Memories of the day she had heard about her parents' death. Memories of the desolation she had felt and the endless number of nights she had cried herself to sleep. Sarah banished her memories and forced herself to concentrate on Ginny. "Why don't you tell me all about it, from the beginning."

"I don't want to," Ginny said sulkily. "If I do, you'll just send me back. And I won't go!" Her voice rose. "I hate that place."

"Let's cross that bridge when we come to it," Sarah said soothingly. "I certainly don't want to send you back to some place you hate."

She knew she was speaking foolishly. She had no choice but to send the girl back to wherever it was she didn't want to go. Someone would be worrying about her.

"I used to live in New York. Then after my parents were . . . in the car accident," Ginny said, trying to keep her voice steady, "I went to live with my uncle—only he didn't want me."

Sarah knew how that felt only too well. She had gone to live with her grandparents. They were elderly and had taken her in out of a sense of duty, nothing more. Her heart swelled with feeling for the little girl across the table from her.

"Are you quite sure your uncle doesn't want you?" she said to Ginny. "Sometimes grownups have a hard time showing what they feel."

Ginny shook her head. "He doesn't want me," she said flatly. "He's busy all the time, and he doesn't have time for a girl."

Sarah was aghast. "Did he actually say that?"

"He didn't have to. After I had been at Five Oaks a few days . . ."

"Five Oaks?" Sarah interrupted. That sounded familiar.

"Five Oaks is my uncle's home. It's sort of a farm in Maryland—only he doesn't grow anything," Ginny explained ingenuously. "He just lives there."

Sarah had heard something about Five Oaks—and recently. It floated around the back of her thoughts but she couldn't capture it. She brought her mind back to Ginny's story.

"After I had been at Five Oaks for a few days, Uncle David said he was sending me away to school. I told him I didn't want to go, but he said I'd be happier there. He said it would be for the best." Ginny's voice began to waver.

Sarah was appalled by the callousness of Ginny's Uncle David. "Perhaps he honestly thought you would be happier at a boarding school," she said, trying to be fair.

Ginny shook her head and tears threatened to spill over. "He just didn't want me. I've told him how much I hate it, but he just keeps saying I have to give myself time."

Sarah's indignation grew. Ginny's Uncle David sounded almost heartless. How could he ignore her cries of unhappiness? Of course she wouldn't be happy in a boarding school. It was obvious Ginny needed a home. Sarah looked at Ginny thoughtfully. The girl's lip was trembling and her eyes were full of tears.

"You need some rest," Sarah said. "Sleeping in the park couldn't have been very comfortable. After that—"

"You aren't going to send me back, are you?" Ginny cried. "You said you wouldn't."

"I said I didn't want to," Sarah pointed out reasonably. "But—"

Ginny burst into tears. "Nobody wants me," she sobbed almost incoherently. "I hate that school. I'll just run away again."

Without thinking, Sarah ran around the table, gathered the sobbing girl into her arms and held her until the sobs eased up a bit. Surely, she was thinking, there had to be another way. If she could get hold of Ginny's uncle and tell him how miserable his niece was, he'd make other arrangements for her. He couldn't be as hard-hearted as Ginny claimed.

Finally Sarah quieted the girl. As she mopped up Ginny's tears she tried to speak firmly. "Listen to me, Ginny. There are a few things I must know. When did you run away?"

"Yesterday afternoon."

"Then you've only been gone a day. When would you have been missed?"

"Last night," Ginny said sulkily. "At dinner."

Sarah held the girl close and stroked her hair. This was going to be the hard part. "You're going to have to tell me your uncle's name, Ginny."

The girl stiffened, but Sarah held her tightly.

"I've got to let him know you're safe. The school has probably notified him, and he'll be worried. You do see that, don't you?"

"He won't be worried, he'll be glad I'm gone," Ginny said spitefully.

Sarah's heart contracted at her words. She spoke with more conviction than she felt. "Of course he won't be glad. He's probably frantic with worry."

Secretly she wasn't sure about that. If Ginny were right, her Uncle David probably regarded his niece's behavior as more of a nuisance than anything else. Still she knew she had to let him know Ginny was all right. "I have to call him," she said again.

"All right," the girl said unwillingly. "But you can tell him I won't go back."

Ginny's voice rose, and Sarah was afraid of another

onslaught of tears. "I'll talk to him," she said sooth-ingly.

She talked for a few more moments until she could feel Ginny begin to relax against her. Strong emotions and a sleepless night were beginning to take their toll. Sarah could feel Ginny growing sleepy.

"You're nice," Ginny murmured drowsily. "Why can't I stay here with you?"

Sarah didn't answer. Instead she held the girl while she thought about her question. Finding Ginny in the park was such a coincidence that it made Sarah wonder. They were alike in so many ways; they shared the same kind of unhappiness. Sarah had suffered just as Ginny was suffering now. Could something like this be strictly a coincidence, she asked herself, or had fate stepped in and taken a hand? Was she destined to help this child? Could Ginny stay with her?

No, she decided. It was impossible. She had a business to run, a life of her own. She couldn't be saddled with a ten-year-old girl—no one would expect her to do such a thing. She had no experience with children and besides, this uncle of hers would probably not allow it.

Sarah felt uncomfortable as she heard her own excuses. After all, she knew from first-hand experience the kind of pain this girl was suffering. She knew the bitterness of feeling unwanted. Who was she to send Ginny away? Sarah jerked her thoughts back to the present. "You'll have to tell me your uncle's name and where I can reach him," she said firmly.

Ginny looked at her so hopefully that Sarah's heart melted and she knew she'd try to keep Ginny with her—for the time being at least. "I'll try to work out something," she promised. "At the very least, I'll try to convince him not to send you back to that school."

Ginny looked at her solemnly, then nodded a little reluctantly. "His name is David de Courcey," she said.

Sarah looked at Ginny in surprise. The pieces of her story were beginning to fall into place. Of course she had heard of David de Courcey. He ran an economic forecasting company and in these times of economic turmoil, she frequently saw his name, or that of his company, in the newspaper. Usually it was on the front page in a news story, but occasionally his name cropped up on the society page as well.

From what Sarah had heard and read, he was something of a genius in the field of economics—not only theoretical economics but also the practical economics of making money. Though she didn't pay much attention to the gossip of her customers, she remembered hearing that he was extremely good-looking and as hard-bitten as they come. From the talk around the shop, she had formed a vague impression of a man with supreme confidence—confidence bordering on arrogance. Everything he touched seemed to turn to gold. And, if the comments she heard were true, his way with women matched his way with money. A number of her single customers, as well as a few married ones, had mentioned the name David de Courcey in wistful tones.

On top of that, he was reputed to be something of a workaholic. It was not an uncommon condition in Washington, D.C., but still, Sarah thought to herself, it hardly made him the type of man to spend much time with a child.

"Do you know his phone number?" Sarah asked.

Ginny gave it to her. "He'll be in his office by now—if he's in the country," she said. "He likes to get to work early."

"Speaking of work," Sarah said, looking at the clock on the wall, "it's after nine. I've got to get ready for work myself."

"Are you leaving?" Ginny sounded genuinely upset at the prospect.

"No," Sarah reassured her quickly. "We came in the

back way so you couldn't see it, but I run a small boutique where I sell the clothes I design. The shop is in the front of my house."

Ginny's eyes lit up. "You design clothes? I'd love to see them."

Sarah laughed. "You will," she promised. "After you've had some sleep."

She led Ginny up to the second floor of her house where there were two bedrooms. A small, third bedroom in the front of the house had been turned into a dressing room for Sarah's customers. Sarah turned down the twin bed in the smaller of the two bedrooms, then tucked Ginny in.

"What about my uncle?" Ginny asked sleepily.

"I'll call him later. Don't worry," Sarah told her. "I'll handle him."

That was a rash promise to make, Sarah told herself as she quickly slipped into an ivory-colored silk skirt and blouse. She chose the clothes instinctively. The ivory silk enhanced the gold tones of her skin and contrasted dramatically with her rich, dark hair. Looking her best always gave her confidence and a measure of poise.

She brushed her shoulder-length hair into a chignon; then she applied mascara and eye liner and subtly shaded her lids with eye shadow. Her large eyes didn't need much in the way of makeup. They were a soft violet color, and Sarah thought they were her best feature. "Arrestingly beautiful," a man from her college years had called them. Even Bill Baker said they were nice.

Sarah looked in the mirror with approval. Simple but elegant was the byword for her working hours. She wanted to be well groomed and attractive but not devastatingly beautiful. It wouldn't do to scare off her customers.

As she dressed, she purposely kept from thinking of David de Courcey. But once she had checked on Ginny and found her sound asleep, she began to worry. Whatever will I say to him? she asked herself as she walked down the stairs and into the part of her house which served as her shop. How can I explain Ginny's unhappiness in a way a man like that can understand?

She glanced at her thin, gold watch and knew she could put it off no longer. Her shop was due to open in half an hour, and she wanted to call him before any customers came in.

Sarah's fingers shook as she punched the numbers on the telephone. She was surprised at how nervous she was. It was because he had been so callous in his treatment of Ginny, Sarah told herself. How was she going to get through to a man like David de Courcey when his niece's obvious unhappiness hadn't touched him in the least?

A secretary answered the phone.

"I'd like to speak to Mr. de Courcey, please," Sarah said firmly. She knew it wouldn't be easy getting through to him. Washington secretaries were famous for protecting their employers from unwanted phone calls.

"Mr. de Courcey is in conference," the secretary said in a bored tone.

Although that was no more than Sarah expected, she was annoyed anyway. "I must speak to him," she said, keeping her voice firm. "It's very important."

"If you'd like to leave your name and number—" the secretary began.

"It's about his niece," Sarah interrupted flatly.

There was silence at the other end of the phone, then the secretary spoke. "Just a moment, please, and I'll get him." All at once she sounded human.

Sarah sighed with relief. She had jumped one hurdle. While she waited for David de Courcey to pick up the phone, her nervousness increased. This busy, important man was not going to like what she had to say about his treatment of Ginny. He was undoubtedly used to people who agreed with him—not people who were critical.

Sarah was aware that she couldn't let him know how she really felt about about his treatment of Ginny . . . she couldn't let him know just how callous and insensitive she found his behavior to be. For Ginny's sake she had to be more tactful than she'd ever been before. She'd have to win over David de Courcey, not lay down the law to him.

After what seemed to be a very long time, someone picked up the phone at the other end of the line. Sarah grasped the receiver more tightly.

"Yes?" a low voice said into her ear.

Another time the voice might have been rounded and slightly mellow. Now it was cold, brusque—and very suspicious. Sarah gulped. This was going to be more difficult than she had feared. Suddenly, she had no idea what to say. She took a deep breath. "I'm calling about your niece, Mr. de Courcey." In her confusion, she forgot to identify herself.

"So I understand from my secretary," he said a little sarcastically. "You may as well know from the beginning that I have no intention of paying for the release of my niece. The police have been notified, and this phone call is being traced."

Sarah was so shocked by his words that she couldn't speak. Did he think she was a—.

"For a kidnapper," he went on coldly and nastily as he completed her thought, "you're certainly inept. Didn't it occur to you that the call was being traced while you were on hold?"

Although his words were infuriating, it was the tone of his voice, arrogant, high-handed and derisive, that ended Sarah's confusion. She found she was growing angry—not because David de Courcey thought she was a kidnapper but because he hadn't yet asked about Ginny. Surely the normal response would be to ask about his niece, not to insult the person he believed to be holding the little girl captive. Her health and happiness obviously were not as important to him as the ransom he had no intention of paying. At that moment Sarah believed David de Courcey to be as unfeeling as Ginny claimed. Anger put words in her mouth.

"I'm not a kidnapper," she said with a quiet and convincing dignity which couldn't help but get through to him. "Nor have I called to demand money for Ginny."

"Then why have you called?" he asked. His voice was still cold and suspicious, but at least he seemed willing to listen.

"I found your niece in Rock Creek Park this morning. She was lying behind some bushes and crying as though her heart would break. Naturally, I took her home with me . . ."

"Naturally," he put in smoothly. "What prompted such an altruistic gesture, Miss . . . if you haven't kidnapped my niece, then perhaps you won't mind telling me your name."

"My name is Sarah Bennet," she snapped. She had the feeling he was making a note of it. "I'll give you my address, too, just in case the trace on this call is inaccurate," she added. In a voice which matched his in coldness, she dictated her address. In the background she could hear his pencil scratch across a sheet of paper as he wrote it down.

"Feel free to have me investigated," she added sweetly.

"Oh, I will," he assured her grimly. "You needn't worry about that."

By this time Sarah definitely did not care for David de Courcey. For one thing he still hadn't asked about Ginny. For another, he sounded overbearing, arrogant and every bit as uncaring as Ginny had said.

"To return to what I was saying," Sarah began coolly. "I took her home with me because—"

"Because," he interposed, "you saw a chance to make some money on the side. A little, judicious blackmail, perhaps?"

That did it. This man was incredible. He didn't seem the least bit interested in what his niece was doing in the park or why she had run away. Sarah gave up trying to hold her temper in check, and she spoke without thinking.

"Really, Mr. de Courcey," she said. Despite the heat of her anger, her voice was icy. "Ginny told me how unfeeling and insufferable you are, but I didn't believe it—until now."

The silence at his end of the phone fairly crackled. Sarah could imagine his anger but she didn't care. She wasn't through yet.

"For your information," she swept on, "Ginny ran away from that dreadful school you put her in. She spent last night in the park. In the park! Do you have any idea how dangerous that was?" Sarah's voice rose. "Do you even care?"

Sarah paused, but there was still no sound from David de Courcey. "If it hadn't been for me, she'd still be in the park—cold, hungry and frightened. Instead she's safe and warm and sleeping in my guest room."

So great was her indignation that her words began to spill out more quickly. "When I call to tell you that Ginny is safe, what do you do? You accuse me of kidnapping, blackmail and heaven knows what else. And not once, not once, Mr. de Courcey, have you bothered to ask about Ginny. You might at least pretend to care."

Sarah stopped suddenly. She had said too much. Her resolution to be tactful had evaporated the moment she had heard his cold and infuriatingly uncaring voice. She had gone too far. David de Courcey would never let Ginny stay with her now. Not after everything she had said. Poor Ginny, Sarah thought. It was easy to see why the little girl was so unhappy.

"Perhaps I owe you an apology," said the voice at the other end of the telephone.

Sarah was not fooled by his words. There was no hint of an apology in his voice. It was as cold as ever. She said nothing, waiting instead to see what he would say next.

"In my experience," he went on, "everyone wants something."

"Not everyone," she put in a little wearily.

"Everyone." His voice was implacable. "I'm used to people who are attracted by the de Courcey name and money. I can spot them a mile off."

"Then I feel sorry for you, Mr. de Courcey," Sarah said evenly. "If you really believe that everyone is after something, you must be as unhappy as Ginny."

"I don't need your pity."

She could tell by the sudden crispness in his voice that she had again made him angry.

"I can protect myself and I intend to protect Genevieve as well. What is it *you* want, Miss . . . uh, Miss Bennet? A payment for rescuing my niece, perhaps?"

Sarah was so furious that she almost hung up on him. This man had a one-track mind! She did not need this kind of aggravation, not now, not ever, she told herself. Then she remembered Ginny sleeping so peacefully, so trustingly upstairs. Ginny was counting on her.

"I don't want or need your money," she said into the receiver. Her voice was tired, as if she had no hope of making him understand.

"Oh, come now, everyone wants a little easy money."

Sarah ignored him. "All I want is for you to understand just how unhappy Ginny really is. At this point in her life, she needs a home, someone to love her, really love her."

"What makes you such an expert on the feelings of my niece?"

Sarah could almost feel his anger over the telephone

line. She grasped the receiver more tightly. "I lost both my parents when I was just about Ginny's age," she said quietly.

"And I suppose you think that gives you the right to interfere in Ginny's life—and mine, too, for that matter."

"No, of course not," Sarah said, trying to sound reasonable. "But it does help me to understand her feelings—which is more than you've bothered to do," she added pointedly.

There was a moment of silence which Sarah made no attempt to break. She didn't suppose many people talked to him that way.

"I'd like to talk to Genevieve," he said finally. It was an order, not a request.

Sarah could tell nothing from his voice, but she doubted that she'd gotten through to him. "Ginny is sleeping," Sarah told him evenly.

Sleeping or not, she had no intention of exposing Ginny to her uncle's wrath. Besides, after everything he had said to her, she wouldn't be human if she didn't take a little pleasure in being able to thwart him, even in such a small way.

"She's completely exhausted, and I do not intend to wake her up. Perhaps you'd like to stop by and see her after she wakes up—if you can fit it into your busy schedule, that is," Sarah finished sweetly.

"I'll be right over," he snapped.

From the tone of his voice, Sarah could tell that it was his turn to try to keep his temper in check. For some reason, the thought cheered her enormously.

"It will take me half an hour or so to get there," he added.

"Ginny will still be sleeping," Sarah told him. "I'm not going to wake her."

He paid no attention. "Half an hour," he said again. It sounded ominously like a warning.

Chapter Two

Mechanically, Sarah set about opening her boutique for the day. Just before she unlocked the door, she checked her reflection in the mirror. Her color was high. Her cheeks were pinker than usual, she noted, and her eyes, normally soft and velvety looking, were sparkling with anger.

Talking to David de Courcey face-to-face was not likely to be any easier than talking to him over the phone, and she knew it. Aside from his insulting accusations and nasty insinuations, there had been an indefinable quality in his voice which made her feel like a cat with its fur stroked backwards. Based on that one conversation, she thought she could never like him. All she was hoping for was a truce.

No, she wasn't looking forward to meeting him. However, for Ginny's sake, she had to try again to keep hold of her temper. For Ginny's sake, she had to make him understand his niece's unhappiness. David de Courcey was not going to get the better of her.

Twenty minutes later, a sleek, silver sports car pulled up in front of her house. Sarah knew at once it belonged to David de Courcey. For once there was a parking space available. Sarah was almost sorry about that. It would have done him good to walk a few blocks, she thought to herself.

From behind a carefully displayed dress in the front window, Sarah watched as Ginny's uncle got out of the car. His looks were the first thing to strike her. He was far better looking than the gossip had led her to believe. Even from a distance, she could tell he was the kind of man who usually got surreptitious second glances from women.

He was tall, a little over six feet, with the ruggedly handsome looks Sarah associated with the West. He was tanned and looked fit—not at all like a man who spent most of his waking hours behind a desk. Sarah wondered if he worked out at a health club.

With a designer's eye, Sarah noted his dark blue suit with approval. It had obviously been made for him by a tailor who knew his work. The fit was exquisite; the suit coat seemed to have been poured over his broad shoulders. He checked the address on her door with a piece of paper in his hand, then started around his car.

Sarah abandoned her position at the window and slipped onto the chair behind her small, antique desk which held her receipts and business records. She felt the desk might give her a psychological advantage of authority. She was, she admitted wryly to herself, going to need every advantage she could think of if she was not to be bested by him. And that was a thing she had no intention of allowing to happen.

The handle of the door turned, and Sarah bent her head over the papers on her desk. David de Courcey stepped inside. Sarah let him wait a moment, then looked up and gave him the impersonal smile with which she greeted unknown customers. "May I help you?" she asked.

His dark enigmatic eyes met hers unwaveringly. Sarah gazed back politely, waiting for him to speak.

"I'd like to see Miss Bennet," he said finally.

She rose and inclined her head slightly. "I'm Miss Bennet. What may I do to help you?"

Let him think she had no idea who he was, she told herself. Though, of course, he could have been no one else. Everything about him—the strong face, the confident carriage of his body, the lift of his head—matched the voice she had heard over the telephone. By pretending not to know him, she was half-hoping to put him on the defensive. After that phone conversation, she had the feeling she was going to need even the slightest advantage in dealing with him.

It didn't work. Sarah hadn't really expected it to. He continued to regard her steadily, almost assessingly. As his eyes flickered over her, Sarah wasn't sure whether or not to be insulted. On occasion, other men had sexually appraised her, but there was nothing sexual in David de Courcey's eyes. She may as well have been a computer he was examining for its capabilities.

His eyes returned to her face. Sarah thought she saw amusement in them. That annoyed her. What had he found in his scrutiny of her that was so funny, she wondered irritably.

"I'm David de Courcey, Genevieve's uncle, as I'm sure you know." The arrogance in his voice annoyed her further.

"Oh? And why is it that I should recognize you?" she asked tartly.

"Who else would I be?" he asked almost flippantly. "You surely don't get many men in here. Besides, my picture has been in the newspaper a number of times."

"Has it?" she asked coolly. "I'm afraid I've missed it." Sarah graciously extended her hand and allowed him to shake it.

"How do you do, Mr. de Courcey?" She asked as though their emotional telephone conversation had never taken place. She intended to show him how poised she could be, and she was determined not to let her temper get the better of her.

When their hands touched, however, she felt a shock which came close to undermining her poise. For a moment she thought he felt it too. Something seemed to flicker at the back of his eyes. Then she withdrew her hand, and she could see only chilly politeness in his face. She had imagined the whole thing, she told herself, though her hand still tingled slightly.

"I was expecting someone considerably older." This time, the appraisal in his eyes was definitely sexual. "That lecture you gave me over the telephone in no way prepared me for the way you look."

Sarah looked at him suspiciously. What was that supposed to mean?

"I had envisioned a much older woman," he went on. "A retired school teacher, perhaps, who had spent her life telling people what to do. Instead I find you're young and beautiful." Once again his eyes swept over her. The enjoyment in them was obvious.

Sarah flushed slightly, more at his words than the way he was looking at her. Had she really sounded like that? Or was it his turn to try to put her on the defensive? If so, he wasn't going to succeed.

"Is Genevieve still sleeping?"

"Yes, she is," Sarah answered calmly. "I checked on her just before I came down."

She gracefully, and gratefully, sank back into her chair. The desk hid her from his eyes—partially at least. He hadn't succeeded in unnerving her . . . yet. But if he continued to look at her like that, he just might.

"Please sit down," she said, gesturing toward one of the spindly, gilt chairs beside her desk.

"How is she, Sarah?" he asked as he balanced on the tiny seat.

She gave him a cool look.

"I hope I can call you Sarah," he added as he noted the expression on her face. "Miss Bennet seems a bit formal under the circumstances."

"Of course . . . David." She emphasized his name slightly. She wasn't going to be put in the position of calling him Mr. de Courcey while he treated her in a more familiar manner. She wasn't his servant, after all.

There was a flash of amusement in his dark eyes. He seemed to know what she was thinking.

"Ginny's exhausted," Sarah said, returning to his question. "Who wouldn't be after spending the night in the park? She was probably too frightened to sleep."

David shifted slightly on the chair. It hadn't been made to comfortably seat a large man. Sarah examined his face carefully. There were circles under his eyes and finely etched lines made more prominent by tiredness. But there was something else in his face that caught at her heart. Something which told her he had been more than worried about Ginny, he had been frightened for her safety.

"You look exhausted, too," she said impulsively.

"I didn't sleep last night either," he confessed. The confession suddenly made him more human. "After the headmistress of Ginny's school called me to tell me of her disappearance, I was up all night worrying . . . thinking of what could be happening to her."

In her mind's eye, Sarah could see him sitting by the telephone; fearful it would ring, fearful it wouldn't, as he waited to hear from what he assumed were Ginny's kidnappers.

"It must have been dreadful for you," she said softly. She was surprised by her words. She was even more surprised to discover that she was beginning to find David likeable. His concern for Ginny certainly seemed sincere enough—now. Sarah found herself making excuses for his behavior over the telephone. He had probably been frantic with worry.

"It was," he replied simply. There was a moment of

bleakness in his eyes as he thought about the night before. He banished it quickly, replacing it with a more businesslike manner.

"Ginny is worth a considerable amount of money," he added.

With his words, some of the sympathy Sarah felt for him dried up. He always seemed to return to the subject of money. She sighed and warned herself not to take him at face value. There was more to this man than met the eye.

"Naturally I assumed she had been kidnapped and when you called this morning, without giving a name, I thought . . ."

"You thought I was the kidnapper," Sarah finished for him dryly. "You've already told me, and in no uncertain terms."

"You do understand, don't you?" he asked.

Sarah realized that his words were close to an apology. She was surprised.

"I was exhausted and terribly worried," he added simply.

"Of course I understand. I'm sure I didn't make things any easier for you." She was trying to be charitable, but still, there was something about him that didn't ring true.

"No, you didn't," he admitted. "Some of the things you said were pretty harsh." He suddenly gave her a smile which lit up his face and eyes. She felt the warmth of his smile, almost as if it were the glow of sunshine.

"I'm sorry," she said a bit vaguely. What was he up to, she wondered. Or was it her turn to be overly suspicious?

He waved her apology away. "It's been an emotional morning for both of us." His eyes were once again appraising. Sarah wondered what in the world he was hoping to find. She was also wondering what had brought about this change in him. An hour earlier he had accused her of everything he could think of. Now he was going out of his way to charm her. Why?

"I'm sure it hasn't been easy for you," Sarah said slowly. Again she warned herself not to be taken in by this man. "But it hasn't been easy for Ginny either."

"Did she tell you why she ran away?" he asked. "Anything specific, that is?"

"She hates that dreadful school you found for her," Sarah said promptly. "I think she wants some kind of home life, some feeling of security. Losing her parents has been a terribly wrenching experience for her. All at once she feels she belongs nowhere, and she feels no one cares for her." Her voice had grown soft and poignant though Sarah didn't realize it.

David's eyes softened, and he looked at Sarah thoughtfully. She was staring out the window as she spoke and didn't see the look on his face. By the time she looked back at him, his mind had returned to Ginny.

"That dreadful school, as you call it," he said wryly, "is the Rock Creek School for Girls, one of Washington's most exclusive schools."

Sarah, however, was not impressed. Many of her customers had children there, and it sounded like a cold, cheerless kind of a place. It might be a prestigious school, but that didn't make it right for Ginny.

"She needs a home," Sarah told him firmly.

"Which I can't give her," David replied. "I have an international consulting company to run, and I have to travel frequently. In fact, I have to leave for London later in the day. I thought a boarding school would be the best place for her. What else could I do?"

The question was rhetorical but Sarah answered it anyway. "You could let someone else do the traveling," she said. Though she tried, she couldn't keep the disapproval out of her voice. Ginny's unhappiness had touched her deeply. "You do have associates, I assume."

"Of course."

"Ginny has only one uncle." All at once the room crackled with animosity. Sarah cursed herself. She didn't want to alienate the man, not when she had seen that he did care for Ginny—in his own way.

"Look," she said urgently, "I'm not judging you. I know your business is important. In many ways the death of Ginny's parents hasn't been fair to you either." The tension in the room eased slightly.

"Couldn't you let her live with you at Five Oaks?" Sarah asked gently, trying to find a compromise. "You could hire a housekeeper to look after her when you're not there."

"What kind of life would that be for a kid?" he said almost angrily. "I spend maybe two nights a week there. The rest of the time I'm out of town or I sleep on the sofa in my office. I'm a busy man."

"And Ginny is a lonely little girl." Once more Sarah knew she had gone too far. It was no good pushing a man like this—he had to be led gently. Sarah took one look at his face and gulped. If she had been an employee of his, she would have been crushed by the look in his eyes.

"As much as I care for her," David snapped, "I can't be expected to devote all my time to Ginny. A business doesn't run itself." He looked around him almost scornfully. "Of course, you wouldn't be able to understand that. Clerking in a dress shop could hardly teach you the ins and outs of big business."

"I happen to own this boutique," Sarah said angrily. She hated being patronized. "Not only do I run it, I create the designs and supervise the seamstresses who make all the clothes in it. I may not know about big business, as you call it, but I do understand the demands a business can make on one's time."

There was grudging respect in his eyes—and also surprise. "Perhaps you do."

"And I also know that no business is worth a little

girl's happiness," she said flatly. For one glorious moment she didn't care if she made him angry.

His eyes flashed. "It's easy for you to say that," he pointed out coldly. "You're not the one being asked to sacrifice years of hard work for the sake of one little girl."

"Neither are you," Sarah said hotly. "I simply said . . ." Her voice trailed off. "This is getting us nowhere. Why don't you let her stay with me, for the time being at least?"

"With you?"

His eyes were suddenly neutral. Sarah had no idea what he was thinking.

"Why would you want her to stay with you?"

"I like her," she replied calmly. She had herself in hand now. "I'd like having her here."

"What about your business?"

"My business isn't nearly as complicated as yours," she answered with saccharin sweetness. "I'm sure I can manage it and look after Ginny at the same time."

He was silent for a moment, apparently mulling over her suggestion. "It might not be such a bad idea," he said finally. "What about school?"

"I thought about that while I was waiting for you to arrive," Sarah told him. She was surprised by his sudden capitulation, but she had no intention of showing it. "There is a public school near here she can attend."

She looked up and caught the expression on his face. Obviously he didn't think a public school was the place for a de Courcey.

"It's a good school," she said quickly. "I know people with children who go there."

"I don't like the idea of sending her to yet another school," he said unexpectedly. "This will be her third school in less than a year."

Sarah looked at him thoughtfully. How she wished she could see into his mind! Earlier that morning she could have sworn his only interest was in the money he thought was involved in Ginny's release. Now he seemed genuinely concerned for her happiness and well-being.

Which reflected the real David de Courcey, she wondered. Probably both, she finally decided. Though she hadn't had a lot of experience with men, she nonetheless judged this one to be rather complicated.

"I can introduce her to a couple of girls who attend the school," Sarah said, going back to his point. She was thinking of the daughters of two of her better customers. "They can help ease Ginny's way."

He shook his head. Sarah was afraid he was going to say no after all. She felt a stab of disappointment and was surprised by its intensity. She leaned across her desk and spoke earnestly.

"Let Ginny stay with me . . . at least through the end of the school year. Then over the summer, perhaps, you and she can work something out."

"Are you sure she won't be in your way?"

"I'm sure," Sarah assured him firmly.

"In that case, I see no reason why she can't stay here pending . . ." All at once he sounded like the businessman she knew he was. The look in his eyes was impersonal, and it chilled her slightly. He could have been setting out the terms of a new contract instead of discussing the welfare of his niece. ". . . pending the completion of an investigation into your background and character."

Sarah gasped with indignation. "You can't be serious."

"I certainly am," he told her a little grimly. "Genevieve is my responsibility. Naturally I'm going to make sure that you are—"

"Fit to look after your niece," Sarah finished with cold anger.

He gave her a measured look. "That is exactly what the investigation will show. What did you expect me to do? Hand Ginny over to you just like that?" He snapped his fingers.

Calm down, calm down, Sarah told herself. What would you do if she were your niece? David was perfectly within his rights, but still . . .

"Do you have something to hide?" He asked coolly. His eyes were hard. "If so, you'd better tell me about it now, because I can guarantee you that it will come out."

"Of course not!" Sarah spoke with the heat of indignation. "It's just that I don't like the idea of someone delving into my life. It's an invasion of my privacy."

He shrugged indifferently, and Sarah had to remind herself that he was acting this way because he cared for Ginny. There was nothing personal involved here.

"You can always change your mind."

Impatiently she shook her head. "If you feel this way, why are you willing to let her stay here with me now?" she wanted to know.

The hardness in his eyes eased slightly. "After meeting and talking to you, I don't expect the investigation to turn up anything . . . untoward. I've made a judgement about you, and my judgement is rarely wrong."

He gave her his sudden smile, but Sarah did not feel like smiling back. Probably he felt he had paid her a compliment, she reflected. If so, it certainly was a backhanded one.

"But I'm still going to have you investigated," he warned. "For my own peace of mind, it has to be done."

Sarah nodded in weary acquiescence although she still didn't like the idea. Her anger was gone, however. Why waste time being angry over something she couldn't change?

"That's settled then." He spoke crisply. "Now, what about room and board? If you'll keep a list of your expenses . . ."

All Sarah's indignation returned in a rush. Really, she thought, there were moments when he could be absolutely insufferable. She had offered to have Ginny as her guest, not as a paying boarder. Was he really so used to buying everything he wanted?

"I think I can handle that myself. Of course, if she eats too much, I can always let you know," she added sarcastically.

It was his turn to be surprised. His eyebrows rose. "Naturally I assumed . . ."

"You assumed wrong," Sarah said flatly. "I told you on the phone this morning that I don't want your money and I meant it. I will let you pay for her clothes, though," Sarah offered with a glint of amusement, "since you're so anxious to pay for something. She probably needs quite a number of things."

"I'm sure she does," he agreed a bit stiffly. "Have the bills sent to my office, and I'll see that they are paid."

Sarah got the idea he wasn't used to having his money refused. "I'll take good care of Ginny," she told him. "You can go to London without worrying. Your niece will be fine."

"Haven't we forgotten one thing?"

"What's that?" Sarah asked apprehensively. What did he have in mind now, she wondered.

"Ginny herself. I don't want her to run away again while I'm out of the country. Will she stay here with you?"

"Why don't you ask her?" From a mirror on the wall, Sarah had caught sight of Ginny standing at the top of the stairs. How long has she been standing there, Sarah wondered. She hoped Ginny hadn't heard her uncle offer her money in return for her keep.

"Ginny," she called. "Come on down. Your Uncle David is here."

Ginny came slowly down the steps and crossed the

room to Sarah's side. She was again wearing Sarah's bathrobe. It dragged along the floor behind her. Her short, light brown hair was tousled, and the expression on her face was so wary that Sarah was sure she had heard nothing of their conversation. She couldn't have known she was to be left with Sarah or she wouldn't have looked so apprehensive. Ginny stood close to Sarah, and Sarah couldn't help being flattered by the girl's trust in her.

David had risen as his niece came down the stairs, but he made no move toward her. Something in his face gave Sarah the fleeting impression that he wanted to reach out to Ginny but he didn't know how.

He sat back down. His face had become unreadable, but Sarah could almost feel him withdraw from Ginny as he sensed her wariness. Sarah's heart swelled with pity for Ginny because she was so alone and for David because he couldn't, or wouldn't, reach out to her.

"I'm not going back," Ginny said stonily. She didn't bother to greet her uncle. She merely said what was uppermost in her mind. "You can't make me."

"Nobody is going to make you do anything," David said. His face had taken on a forbidding look, and his voice was cool.

Sarah put her arm around Ginny and found the little girl was trembling. She looked from Ginny's defiant face to David's closed-in expression and decided it was up to her to take the initiative.

"Your Uncle David and I have been talking about letting you stay here," Sarah said gently.

The defiance in Ginny's face was replaced almost instantly by happiness and relief.

"Can I stay forever?" she asked.

Sarah laughed. "Perhaps not that long. But at least until the end of the school year."

"Then I won't have to go back to that awful place?"

"No, you'll go to a school down the street."

Ginny threw her arms around Sarah's neck and hugged her tightly. "I knew you'd want me. I just knew it," she crowed.

"It's all thanks to your uncle," Sarah said. Through the child's excitement, she could feel David's silence. It filled the room.

Gently she pushed Ginny away, and they both turned to face him. For a moment Sarah thought she saw a flicker of bitterness at the back of his eyes, but she told herself she was wrong. Hadn't he told her himself that he didn't have enough time to devote to Ginny?

"Thank you for not sending me back to that school, Uncle David," Ginny said politely.

"Do you think you'll be happy with Miss Bennet?" he asked.

"Oh yes. It will be like having a home again."

David got to his feet. "I have to go to London for a few days," he told his niece. "I'll call you when I get back."

"Have a nice trip," she said as politely as before. Obviously, she had nothing more than a dutiful affection for him.

Sarah sent Ginny back upstairs to change, then she walked David to the door. "Don't worry about her," she urged him.

She felt distinctly uncomfortable. She wished she hadn't witnessed the scene between Ginny and David. Polite though they both were, there had been unexpressed frustration and unhappiness on both their parts. "She'll be fine."

"I can see that," he answered. The bitterness was suddenly out in the open. "You seem to have accomplished more in a few short hours than I've done in months."

Sarah stared up at him, not knowing what to say. For an awful moment she sensed the bleakness he must have been feeling. Though Ginny hadn't exactly rejected him, she hadn't been forthcoming either.

Then Sarah reminded herself that David was responsible for the way Ginny treated him. *He* had sent her off to school against her wishes. *He* had ignored her cries of unhappiness. *He* was the one who was too busy to spend any time with her. Still, Sarah's tender and susceptible heart ached for him. Perhaps he simply didn't know how to show love. Before she could say anything, he yanked open the door and stalked out to his car.

Sarah suppressed a sudden longing to follow him and put her arms around him in comfort as she had done with Ginny. She wanted nothing more than to draw his head upon her breast and stroke his hair. Hurriedly, she closed the door behind him. She was shaken by his bitterness, but she was even more shaken by her response to it.

At five o'clock Sarah straightened her desk and prepared to close her small shop for the day. She was tired and it seemed like there had been twice as many hours in the day as usual. It certainly seemed like a long time since morning.

In between customers and fittings, Sarah had made arrangements to have a couple of girls come over on Sunday afternoon to meet Ginny. She had also called Bill and cancelled their date for the evening.

It had occurred to her that Ginny might be the perfect excuse for ending a relationship that had continued more out of habit than anything else. Somewhat reluctantly, she had agreed to let Bill take Ginny and her to dinner the next night. She wasn't sure just how deeply Bill cared for her, but she didn't want to hurt him.

Throughout the afternoon of phone calls and customers, thoughts of the responsibility she had undertaken hammered away at her. Through sheer impulsiveness, she had allowed herself to get caught up in the lives of two unhappy people. Ginny's unhappiness was obvious; and Sarah felt David's unhappiness instinctively. Despite his success, his money and his charm, she believed he was lonely. She was also sure he didn't realize it himself. So, because of the affinity she felt for Ginny and the attraction she had felt for her uncle . . . Here Sarah stopped. Had she been attracted to David de Courcey? He had angered her, infuriated her and moved her to pity. His smile had fluttered her heart.

She switched off the lamp on her desk and sat in the dim light of evening for a few moments. Yes, she finally told herself, she was attracted to David. She might as well admit it. David. With his forceful personality and magnetic smile, he was undoubtedly more than part of the reason she had decided to end her suddenly tedious relationship with Bill.

Face it, Sarah told herself, David de Courcey is an exciting man. The kind of man she had only half-consciously wished for that morning. Was it only that morning that restlessness had sent her into the park? Sarah asked herself wryly as she left the shop and went into the kitchen. It seemed like days had gone by, since morning.

"Are you ready?" Ginny asked. She was sitting at the table reading a fashion magazine.

"I will be in a few minutes," Sarah replied. "I just want to go upstairs and . . ."

"You're not going to change, are you?" Ginny looked at her admiringly. "You look perfect just like that."

Sarah couldn't help but be flattered. "No, I'm not going to change. I just need to get my pocketbook and car keys."

She had promised to take Ginny to Bloomingdale's for some new clothes. Though Sarah naturally preferred her own boutique to any department store, she knew that kids Ginny's age found the place fascinating.

"We're going to be having dinner with a friend of

mine tomorrow night," Sarah said as they drove out Wisconsin Avenue.

"A boyfriend?" Ginny asked suspiciously.

"No, not a boyfriend." Sarah mimicked her tone. "Just a friend."

"Do you have a boyfriend?" Ginny then asked.

Sarah laughed a little uncomfortably. "No, I don't."

"Why not?" Ginny wanted to know. She stared at Sarah critically. "You're so pretty."

"There's White Flint," Sarah said, pointing to the large suburban Maryland shopping center which housed some of Washington's more glamourous department stores.

"I see Bloomingdale's," Ginny squealed.

She had momentarily forgotten Sarah's love life, and Sarah was just as glad. That was a line of questioning she definitely didn't want to pursue.

Hours later, they staggered back out to Sarah's car. In their arms were stacked boxes of clothing. They giggled like teenagers as they drove back to Georgetown. Though Sarah had enjoyed herself, she was beginning to realize that looking after a ten-year-old girl wasn't going to be easy. And her self-imposed task of bringing Ginny and David together was going to be even more difficult, she thought with sudden seriousness.

However, a look at Ginny's face, relaxed and smiling in the reflected light of a traffic signal, convinced her she had been right in keeping Ginny with her. She shook off her seriousness.

A few moments later they were crowning their evening with rich, gooey sundaes at an old-fashioned ice cream parlor near Sarah's house.

Chapter Three

Wearily, Sarah put down the telephone. The day had consisted of one crisis after another. One of her seamstresses was sick, a bolt of specially ordered fabric had arrived flawed and an old and valued customer had picked out a dress for that very evening which needed several alterations. With a seamstress sick, Sarah wasn't sure how it would all work out.

She pushed her hands through the cascades of hair she had left down that morning and sighed. Once she had loved these challenges; a crisis used to send her adrenalin pumping. Now all she felt was tired. She was thinking of closing her shop on Saturday and taking Ginny to the beach for the weekend. Sarah loved the beach and it had been years since she'd been there, years since she felt she could take a weekend off.

The door to her shop opened.

"Have you seen this?" Ginny cried without bothering to say hello. She was waving a copy of the morning newspaper. Sarah winced. She had seen it and had hoped that Ginny wouldn't.

Ginny didn't wait for an answer. She rushed over to Sarah's desk and unfolded the paper. There, on the front page of the style section, was a picture of David de Courcey, looking more handsome than Sarah remembered him, in a well-cut dinner jacket. Close beside him stood a gorgeous, unidentified blonde who had been poured into a strapless, black sheath dress. Her arm was linked through David's, and the camera had caught the proprietary look in her eye.

"It says Uncle David was at a reception at the French embassy last night," Ginny said as she pointed to the caption under the picture. "That means he's back from London, and he didn't even bother to call me like he said he would."

Sarah looked up at the little girl in concern. Ginny seemed near tears. To her it was just one more bit of proof that her uncle didn't care for her even though she had been cool, almost cold when she last saw him, Sarah had been afraid of this kind of reaction. That's why she had hidden the morning's paper from her.

"I'm sure he'll call soon," she said comfortingly. "He's probably been very busy. You know how important his business is to him."

"It's more important than I am," Ginny sniffed. The tears were definitely threatening to spill over now. "But not more important than that woman."

Sarah folded up the newspaper and put it in the wastebasket under her desk. "I'm sure he'll call this weekend," she said.

Ginny gave her a cynical glance which twisted at Sarah's heart. And if he doesn't call, I'll call him, Sarah vowed to herself. For Ginny's sake. "How was school?"

Ginny made a face. "Terrible."

Sarah knew she didn't mean it. Though she was still

in her first week at her new school, it seemed to suit her very well.

"Anne asked me to come for dinner and spend the night," Ginny said, naming one of the girls to whom Sarah had introduced her. "Can I?"

Sarah frowned. "On a school night? I don't think so."

"Oh, I forgot to tell you." Ginny was offhand. "We don't have school tomorrow. The teachers are having some kind of meeting."

"In that case, I think it's all right for you to go."

Ginny's face lit up.

"About this weekend . . ." Sarah went on. Suddenly she felt an overwhelming desire to get away—from the noise of the city, from the pressures of her job, from everything. She could practically feel the warmth of the sun on her face and the sea breeze as it came in off the water. It had been so long since she had been to the beach that she had almost forgotten how much she loved it. Almost, but not quite. Now it all came back to her.

"One of the other girls at school is having a birthday party on Saturday, and she asked me to come," Ginny was saying.

Reluctantly Sarah brought her thoughts back from the beach.

"Is it all right if I go?"

"A birthday party?" Sarah asked, trying not to show her disappointment. So much for her weekend at the beach.

"Carolyn, the girl who is having the party, said her mother will call you and tell you all about it. Is it okay?"

"I think so," Sarah said, "but I want to talk to Carolyn's mother before I decide." She was suddenly very conscious of her responsibility of Ginny—and to David.

"I'm going to pack my nightgown and stuff," Ginny said. "Anne said to come over as soon as I could."

"Go ahead," Sarah told her.

Ginny turned and skipped joyfully out of the room, letting the door slam behind her as she went. Sarah stared after her ruefully. It's better this way, she told herself. She had plenty of work to do at the shop, and she was behind in some of her designs. There would be other weekends.

Sarah subdued the restlessness which seemed to be affecting her more and more frequently and pulled a large, black accounting ledger from the bottom drawer of her desk. That would keep her mind off the beach!

A few minutes before five, she began to close her shop. She was upstairs in the fitting room when the bell over the door tinkled. One last customer, she told herself as she hurried downstairs. She stopped in the doorway. Instead of a woman looking through the displays of clothing, David de Courcey seemed to be filling her small shop. He stood in the middle of the room looking more masculine than ever amidst the feminine trappings.

At the sight of him, Sarah's heart made an unexpected leap. She had to remind herself that she was angry with him for not getting in touch with Ginny sooner. That reminder, however, did nothing to slow the surge of gladness she was feeling.

Sarah moved just inside the door. There, David's eyes stopped her. As he had done only six days before, he let his eyes wander from her face to her graceful neck, to the soft curves of her breasts under the bright pink silk of her dress. Sarah felt her heart start to race. This was completely unlike the way he had looked her over before. Before she might as well have been a machine. Now he was looking at her as a man looks at a woman. His eyes, as they slid to her slender waist and curving hips, were making her very aware of her femininity. They were also making her angry. He had no right to look at her, or any woman, like that.

"Welcome home," she said coolly. "When did you get back?" She tried to avoid an accusing tone though she was as aware of the newspaper picture of him in the wastebasket near her feet as she was of his promise to call Ginny as soon as he got back to town . . . his broken promise.

"I got back yesterday afternoon." He didn't seem to notice her coolness. He walked across the shop and sat down in the chair behind her desk. He smiled up at her.

It was the smile Sarah had seen so many times in her mind's eye during the past week. It was a charming smile, filled with a gentle warmth.

"How is Ginny?" he asked.

"She missed you," Sarah told him. Wanting to do something other than stand still while his eyes scanned her face and body, Sarah began straightening things for the next day.

"I find that a little hard to believe," he said. "When I left her last Friday, I had the idea she didn't care if she ever saw me again."

"That was just an act. She's afraid of being hurt. She thinks you don't want anything to do with her," Sarah added flatly.

David frowned, and she could see he was irritated by her frankness. "Is she here?" he asked. "I'd like to take the two of you to dinner."

"Oh, she'll be so disappointed! She's spending the night with a new friend," she explained. "If only you'd called. She just left a few minutes ago."

"Tonight is a school night," David said disapprovingly. "Is that how you look after her?"

Sarah was nettled even though she had asked much the same thing. "Tonight is not a school night," she corrected him. "The students have tomorrow off." Sarah looked at him doubtfully. "Perhaps I should call her, and tell her you're here. I know she'll be disappointed at not seeing you."

"No, don't do that. I'm glad she is making friends so easily. I'll take her to lunch tomorrow, instead. Do you think she'd like that?"

"I think she'd like almost any attention from you."

He ignored that. "Now, what about dinner?"

"I just told you. Ginny is at a friend's house . . ."

He interrupted her. "I know. Will you have dinner with me?"

Sarah's first impulse was to refuse him. She gestured around her. "Thank you, but I don't think I should. I have some work to do here and . . ."

"It can wait," he said authoritatively. "I want you to have dinner with me."

Sarah stiffened. He had turned the dinner invitation into an order.

David must have felt her annoyance. "Please," he added, softening his tone and giving her a look she found hard to refuse.

Still, she hesitated. Was she afraid of going to dinner with him? she asked herself. Was she afraid of becoming involved with such a vital, forceful male?

"I wish you'd say yes," he said persuasively.

Sarah was almost undone by the warmth of his eyes. He genuinely wanted her, Sarah Bennet, to have dinner with him. Not the beautiful blonde of the newspaper picture, but her. And, he was actually coaxing her to accept. Sarah was flattered in spite of herself.

Why not? she asked herself. Hadn't she been wishing for more glamour, more excitement in her life? Now that it was offered to her, she would be foolish to push it away. Sarah laughed aloud, all at once feeling carefree. "All right," she said, giving in suddenly. "I'd like to have dinner with you."

He stood abruptly and looked down at her. "Wonderful," he said softly.

Sarah's spirits soared. Their eyes met and she felt something warm and electric flow between them. Then his eyes seemed to cloud over. His next words broke the spell.

"We can talk about Genevieve," he said. "I have an idea I'd like to discuss with you."

Sarah's heart plummeted. Of course that was the reason behind the dinner invitation. She had been foolish to think he wanted her company. He had his unidentified blonde for company.

"We really don't need to go out to talk about Ginny," Sarah said coolly. "We can talk here."

"Of course we can. But I'd like to take you to dinner. I'll pick you up at seven-thirty. That will give you a couple of hours to get ready."

Again his voice was dictatorial, and Sarah was nettled. If he thought that she was going to spend the next two hours getting ready for dinner with him, then he was wrong!

"That's fine," she said aloud. Though she spoke sweetly, she wanted him to know just how wrong he was. "That will give me just enough time to get some work done."

"Fine. I'll see you then."

With a frown on her face, Sarah watched him leave the shop. What was there about him that caused such mixed feelings in her? He annoyed her, he angered her. Yet at the same time, she found him very attractive and appealing. Though his arrogance infuriated her, she could also feel sorry for him. She hadn't forgotten the look on his face when he had left her shop last week or the strength and intensity of her desire to comfort him.

Sarah dressed carefully. Dinner with David was not likely to be in one of the casual Georgetown spots Bill favored. She slipped into a dress of lavender silk, luxuriating in the feel of the fabric against her bare skin. The slender straps which held up the snug bodice meant a strapless bra which she hated. Instead, she went without and enjoyed the whisper-soft feel of the fabric against her breasts and thighs. The skirt, cut on the bias, swirled gently around her whenever she moved.

Intently Sarah stared at herself in the full-length mirror on the back of her door. Her dark hair fell gently to her shoulders, and the lavender of the dress made her violet eyes luminous. She had rarely looked better, she decided, though it didn't matter. David probably wouldn't even notice.

To her surprise, he did notice after all. As Sarah opened the door the look in his eyes made her knees go weak. Hurriedly she stepped outside and closed the door behind her.

David took her arm and steered her toward his sleek, silver sports car. Deftly he settled her in the plush bucket seat.

"You said you have an idea for Ginny," Sarah said without preamble as David started the car. "What is it?"

The look in his eyes had brought warmth to her face but the touch of his hand did more than that. It jolted her. She began to regret having accepted his dinner invitation. Honestly, she told herself, first you wish for excitement and glamour, and then when it finally comes your way, you want to run and hide. She was disgusted with herself.

"Let's wait until we get to the restaurant before we talk about Ginny," he was saying. "There's no rush, is there?"

"I do have to work tomorrow," she told him stiffly.

"So do I. I won't keep you out late," he promised. He turned and gave her a long look. Even in the twilight Sarah was sure he could see that she wore virtually nothing beneath her dress. His face had such a knowing look that Sarah was annoyed as well as embarrassed.

"You look lovely," he said. "Is that dress one of your own designs?"

"Yes, it is."

"You're the perfect advertisement for the clothing you design."

"Thank you." Sarah was pleased. A warmth stole through her body, dispelling the annoyance and helping her to relax.

"I thought we'd have dinner in the country," he said, mentioning the name of a very popular inn nestled in the rolling Virginia countryside.

Sarah was impressed in spite of herself. She'd never been there, but she'd heard of it.

"On nights like this," he added, "they set up a few tables outside. It's very romantic." He gave her a warm look.

Sarah wasn't sure she liked the sound of that or why he had bothered to arrange a romantic evening for the two of them. "How did you manage to get reservations on such short notice?" she asked, bringing the conversation to a more practical level. "I've always heard you have to call two weeks ahead."

"Most people do," he said casually. "But I've always found that a little judicious tipping works wonders."

Sarah stared out her window as they left the city behind. No wonder he thought money could solve every problem. For him it always had—until Ginny came along.

"Would you like some music?" Without waiting for an answer, he filled the car with soft music.

Sarah leaned back in her seat and let herself enjoy the music and the beauty of the evening.

The restaurant, at the end of a long narrow road, was nestled amidst tall, sheltering trees. They were taken around the side to a large expanse of lawn bordered by shrubs and tubs of spring flowers. As David had promised, cloth-covered tables were sprinkled across the lawn.

Their table was at the edge of the lawn, slightly away from everyone else. Sarah gave David a suspicious look. What was he up to?

"What do you think?" he asked. "Isn't this lovely? We might as well be alone."

"It's lovely," Sarah admitted grudgingly. Instead of the conversation of other diners, she could hear nothing but the chirping of crickets. It was dark except for the soft light of candles and the stars which were just beginning to show in the sky. To say this was romantic was something of an understatement, Sarah thought to herself.

"I just don't know what we're doing here," she said aloud.

"Of course you do," he said, giving her a warm and knowing look.

He leaned over and captured her hand. Sarah felt her hand tingle as he gently caressed it.

"Isn't this what you wanted?" he asked as his thumb brushed back and forth across her skin.

Sarah snatched her hand away. "I want to talk about Ginny," she said stiffly. "I thought that was why we came."

"Of course we did—but only in part."

The waiter arrived with menus for both of them, calling a halt to their conversation. Sarah stared at the menu without seeing what was written there. What was it he thought she wanted? She blushed as she realized he must have noticed the fact that she found him attractive. That wasn't the kind of thing that could be hidden from a man like David de Courcey. He knew women far to well not to realize what the heightened color in her face meant. No more, Sarah vowed. She had to get a grip on her emotions—a tight grip if she knew what was good for her.

After they had ordered, the waiter brought over two green-stemmed glasses filled with what looked like champagne. Swirled through the champagne was a dark pink liquid.

"Our special cocktail—framboise and champagne," the waiter said. "Compliments of the house."

Sarah received her cocktail in silence. How many women did he bring here, she was wondering. He must come frequently if he rates cocktails on the house.

David silently touched his glass to hers, choosing to let his eyes speak for him. Sarah stared back at him suspiciously, trying not to show the twinges of panic she was beginning to feel. Why is he so determined to turn this into a romantic evening? she asked herself wildly. What's going on in his mind?

"About Ginny," she began. She was appalled to find her voice sounding weak. She took a sip of her cocktail.

"I'd rather talk about you."

Sarah's suspicions increased, and so did her feeling of panic. She simply didn't trust him. He had some reason for this sudden romancing. She didn't believe for a moment that he was attracted to her.

"I still don't understand why you want to have Ginny stay with you."

Sarah stiffened. "I told you that before. She reminds me a little of myself, and I'd like to help her if I can."

"There has to be more to it than that," he persisted. "You're a woman with a successful, demanding career. Why would you want to take on the responsibility of a girl you don't know. It doesn't make sense."

"It makes perfect sense to me," Sarah returned coolly. "I'm sorry if you can't understand it, but there it is."

"There has to be more to it than meets the eye . . ."

"Why do you insist on looking for things that aren't there?" Sarah broke in.

She was suddenly angry. Her voice rose, and she thought it was fortunate the other diners weren't nearby. In another moment she and David would be arguing.

He, too, was annoyed. "I'm looking for another reason, because in my experience, there usually is one. Things are seldom as simple as they seem. Take your case, for example. You're an ambitious woman. You must expect to get something out of this situation. It's not money—at least not the kind of money I've offered you so far. If it's not money, then what is it?"

Sarah was furious, so furious she could barely speak. Even now, he refused to believe she had only Ginny's interests at heart. What had made him so cynical? "I feel sorry for you," she told him in a voice filled with deadly cold. That, she noticed with satisfaction, seemed to take him aback.

"Oh, and why is that?" he asked in a voice which matched her own.

"Because you seem to think that everything, even love, has a price. You can't conceive of anything being done unselfishly or out of simple kindness. Everything has to have an ulterior motive."

"In my experience . . ." he began.

"Your experiences have obviously been pretty warping," Sarah snapped.

David didn't answer, and Sarah immediately regretted her words. She stole a look at him and thought his face looked strained. She had hurt him. Remorse swept over her. Perhaps his experiences in life had indeed been warping, she thought miserably. She didn't stop to analyze why she was suddenly so concerned about his feelings.

"I'm sorry," she said gently. "It's just that your cynicism is a little . . . overwhelming at times."

"There's no need to apologize," he said curtly. "For all your success, you're still very young. When you've grown up a little more, you'll see how right I am." His tone was arrogant, even patronizing.

Sarah felt her anger return. I needn't have worried about hurting him, she told herself scornfully. He's so conceited, he's impervious to anything he doesn't want to hear—even if it is the truth.

To Sarah's relief, the waiter arrived with the first course. They sat in silence as he set small plates filled with shrimp and crab in front of them and opened and poured the crisp, white wine. This time there was no silent toast, no clinking of glasses.

"I've had an idea for what to do with Ginny this summer," he said finally.

"She can stay with me," Sarah said quietly. She was determined not to let him goad her into losing her temper again.

"She can't stay with you forever," he pointed out. "That's hardly fair to you. Especially since you have refused to let me pay you—so far that is."

He is insufferable, Sarah thought though she refused to rise to the bait. "You can't send her to camp or school for the summer," she said warningly. "Ginny would be miserable."

"I have a house at the beach," he told her. "Ginny can spend the summer there."

"She'll need someone to look after her. I suppose you can hire someone for that," Sarah said witheringly.

"Actually, I was thinking of you."

"Me!" Sarah was astonished. "I can't spend the summer at the beach. I have a business to run."

"Surely you can find someone to look after your shop."

"There's far more to it than that," Sarah said indignantly. "I just can't walk away from my business for the summer. It's impossible."

"I thought you cared about Ginny." His voice was almost a sneer. "I thought you wanted to help her."

Sarah stared at him in confusion. "I do, but . . ."

He shrugged. "Not enough, apparently."

"It's you who should spend more time with her," Sarah cried. "I'm just a stranger she met in the park one day. If you'd give her the love and attention she needs, she wouldn't have to turn to someone like me."

He shrugged again. "I'm willing to give her what time I can this summer, but I'm not willing to take off the entire summer. I couldn't even if I wanted to. I've got commitments, obligations."

"What about your obligation to Ginny?" Sarah asked with deadly calm.

He looked annoyed. "I admit I have an obligation to Ginny—an obligation I'm trying to fulfill."

"By breaking a promise to her?" Sarah asked.

He looked taken aback. "What promise have I broken?"

"You promised to call her as soon as you got back from London. You didn't."

"I got back yesterday evening," he said coldly, "and I stopped by to see her less than twenty-four hours later. Is that breaking a promise?"

"Ginny thinks so."

David expelled a deep breath in exasperation. "I was busy. Surely she didn't expect me to call from the airport."

Sarah ignored his last comment. "You weren't too busy to call that blonde woman you took to the French embassy last night," she told him trying to keep her voice indifferent.

He was silent for a moment. "You saw the picture in the paper," he said finally.

"Yes."

"I suppose you showed it to Ginny."

"Certainly not. In fact, I hid it from her. Someone at school showed it to her."

David looked at her so intently that Sarah felt her face grow warm. What was he looking for? Whatever it was, he seemed to find it.

"You're jealous," he said triumphantly.

"Jealous!" Sarah was aghast. "I am no such thing."

He gave her a complacent look. "I know women. You're jealous."

Sarah was so infuriated by his smugness that she could have hit him. "Your conceit knows no limits," Sarah said through clenched teeth. The worst part of it was that she had been a little jealous when she saw the picture. He was right about that. "I don't think there is anything more to be said," Sarah said icily. "I'd like to go home."

He looked surprised. "We haven't had dessert yet."

"Nevertheless, I'd like to go home. If you won't take me, I'll call a taxi."

"I must have struck a nerve," he observed as he signalled for the waiter.

Sarah ignored him.

The ride back to town was accomplished in complete silence. It wasn't until they reached her house that Sarah spoke. "You needn't get out."

David paid no attention. He parked the car, then walked her to her door. Sarah opened it and was annoyed to find David had followed her inside.

"It's been a long day, and I'm tired," she said, trying to retain her composure. All at once, she was sick of him. "I'd like you to leave."

"We still haven't decided what to do about this summer." He went into her small sitting room and sat down without waiting for an invitation. Sarah followed helplessly.

"I've already told you. I can't close my shop for the summer," she said tiredly.

"Then find someone to run it for you," he said smoothly.

Talking to him was like talking to the wall, she thought. He was impervious to everything she had to say.

"At least think about it," he urged her. He gave her his sudden smile, and Sarah felt he was trying to charm her. But it was too late for that. That might have worked earlier, but not now.

"It would mean so much to Ginny—and to me." The words were accompanied by a warm look.

Sarah glared at him. "I'll think about it," she said, hoping he would leave. Much to her relief, he stood up.

"Don't you find that looking after Ginny restricts your love life?" His question was so casual that it took Sarah a moment to absorb it.

"My love life?" she echoed blankly. If his investigation of her had been as thorough as he claimed it would be, surely he realized she had no love life. "Oh, you mean Bill Baker."

"That is exactly who I mean." David's eyes narrowed. "I don't want him spending the night with you as long as Ginny is here."

"Bill has never spent the night here," Sarah retorted indignantly. "Not that it's any of your business."

"You're wrong. As long as Ginny is here, it's very much my business. You're a grown woman. What you do is your own affair—except where it concerns my niece."

"I'm beginning to think your investigation of me wasn't as thorough as you seem to think it was. For one thing, Bill and I are no longer seeing one another. For another thing . . ." She broke off. What was the use? He could think what he wanted. Nothing she could say would change his mind. Then she noticed David staring at her thoughtfully.

"I see," he said slowly and meaningfully.

It was obvious he had jumped to some conclusion, but what that conclusion was, Sarah didn't know.

"I'm beginning to see very clearly." His words obviously had meaning for him, but they made no sense at all to Sarah. "That leaves you free for some other man."

In a matter of seconds, he had crossed the room and

taken her in his arms. Sarah was too surprised to protest as his lips took possession of hers. For a moment she felt only the warmth of his mouth, then she began to struggle to get free. David ignored her struggles. This wasn't what she wanted, she cried to herself, though her body was beginning to tell her otherwise. In desperation, Sarah tried to move her lips from his.

"Don't," she started to say, but it was a mistake. He immediately took advantage of the way her lips parted and invaded her mouth with his tongue. Sarah felt her body betray her as his tongue lightly caressed the sensitive skin of her mouth. Her knees turned to jelly and her hands stopped trying to push him away. Instead they seemed to wind around his neck of their own volition.

As his tongue began to probe more deeply, more insistently, Sarah abandoned her struggles completely. Though she didn't quite realize it, she melted against him, letting his hands press her close. He lifted his lips for a moment. "That's better," he muttered.

Sarah opened her eyes partially. His face was unreadable except for the desire Sarah saw written there. That was plain to see. She shivered, half in anticipation, half in apprehension. Her eyes moved to his lips and she watched them as they slowly came closer to hers. As she watched his seductive mouth move closer and closer, she began to feel a heat coursing through her body. This time when his lips touched hers, they parted willingly.

The kiss lengthened and intensified until time disappeared. Sarah leaned against David, mesmerized by the workings of his mouth and the movement of his hands. He was no longer gripping her tightly. Instead he was caressing her with a deliberate sensuousness that was sending fire through her veins.

When his mouth left hers and traveled slowly down to her throat, Sarah felt her skin was being seared by his touch. He lifted his hand and brushed it across her breasts. As Sarah felt her nipples grow taut in response, the world began to spin crazily. Although her eyes were closed, there seemed to be bright bursts of color everywhere.

Her head fell back and his lips moved down her shoulders toward her breasts. Sarah could feel them straining against the tight fabric of her dress. Before David, no man had ever caused such feelings of sweet delirium, no man had ever made her body burn like this. No man had ever gotten close enough even to try.

Sarah's sense of propriety had vanished, leaving her warm and pliant in his arms. Under the magic of his hands and mouth, she had become a desirable and ardent woman. Nothing else seemed to matter.

It was David who restored her sanity. His lips moved back to hers for a long lingering kiss. Then he lifted his head a few inches. His eyes glittered as he spoke. "We're alone. Ginny won't be back until morning." His lips began tickling the lobe of her ear. "We have the whole night before us," he breathed.

Sarah shivered at the passion in his voice. Then, as the meaning of his words sunk in, she stiffened. For some reason, the photograph of David and the statuesque blonde from the morning's paper popped into her mind. Last night David had probably been in her bed—tonight he wanted to be in Sarah's.

Her eyes widened with shock, and she pushed him away. Surprised, he reached for her, but Sarah took a few unsteady steps backward and took hold of a nearby chair. She needed it partially for support and partially as a barrier.

His eyes narrowed. She stared at him, not knowing what he was thinking. She took deep steadying breaths of air as she tried desperately to get her own thoughts in order. Never had she let her body get so out of control. Never had she let a man . . . Sarah's mind shied away from what had just taken place.

"What was that all about?" she asked shakily.

"I might ask you the same thing," he returned icily.

She stared at him unbelievingly. "You were trying to seduce me!" Her voice was soft but accusing.

David made an impatient gesture with his hand. "I wasn't trying to seduce you. From what I saw and felt tonight, you're long past that anyway. I was trying to make love to you. I thought that was what you wanted."

"Why?" Sarah wanted to know. "Haven't I made it clear to you that I am not interested in you, except for Ginny's sake?"

He answered her question indirectly. "I can't figure you out." His breathing had returned to normal, and he seemed to have forgotten the intensity of what had taken place between them. He sounded almost casual, indifferent.

Sarah knew that she would never forget the feelings he had stirred in her—not if she lived to be one hundred. They were too intense, too searing, too . . . Resolutely she made herself listen to his words. She made herself assume his indifference.

"You keep saying you want nothing for looking after Ginny, but I find that very hard to believe. Since it's not money you want, I thought it might be me."

She began to laugh. She couldn't help herself. The gall of the man was overwhelming.

"You wouldn't be the first woman who has tried trickery to get my attention," he pointed out. "Nor will you be the last."

"You do like to think the worst of people," Sarah observed caustically. "And your arrogance, is beyond belief."

He didn't seem to care what she thought. "You were right about one thing," he said suddenly. "The investigation of you wasn't as thorough as I had been led to believe." He lowered his voice. "You're a very responsive woman. You've obviously had some experiences that my investigators missed."

Sarah couldn't help herself. She stepped away from the protection of the chair and slapped him with all her strength. His arrogance was one thing, his blindness was another. Couldn't he see that he was the first, the only man to stir her in that way? Wasn't it obvious that he alone could provoke such a passion?

David's hands closed over her shoulders, and for a moment Sarah was afraid he was going to hit her back. Instead he kissed her again and Sarah was powerless to resist. It was a hard, bitter kiss, and it hurt her far more than a slap would have.

She jerked herself free and stared at him with angry reproachful eyes.

"Tell Ginny I'll pick her up at eleven tomorrow morning," David said. A moment later he was gone.

Chapter Four

"Sarah! *Sarah!*" called Ginny. She ran into the shop and flung herself onto the delicate, gold chair near Sarah's desk.

Sarah gave Ginny a searching look, then a relieved smile. Apparently the lunch with her uncle had gone well. Sarah had been afraid that the girl would come back subdued and unhappy. Instead, she had never seen her quite so excited.

"Uncle David says we're going to spend the summer at the beach," Ginny announced. She bounced up and down in excitement. "And he says you're going, too."

Sarah was completely taken aback. The smile faded from her lips. She had told David no such thing. She had said she'd think about it, nothing more. And she had thought about it. She'd thought of nothing else since David had left last night.

Before he had taken her in his arms, her reasons for not going to the beach were impersonal ones, based on her business. The feel of his lips on hers had changed that. Now her reasons were intensely personal. She knew she couldn't live under the same roof as David. That would be sheer folly. He had called her a responsive woman. And, all of a sudden, she was just that. A woman responsive for the first time to the touch of a man. Spending the summer at David's beach house was out of the question. But how was she going to explain that to Ginny?

Sarah looked past Ginny to see David quietly entering her shop. Their eyes met briefly, taking Sarah back to what had happened the night before. For a moment Ginny was forgotten as Sarah relived those few moments of passion. She could see that David, too, was remembering the electricity which had flowed between them. Then his face grew blank. Sarah pulled herself up short and gave him what she hoped was a reproving look. He had no right to tell Ginny that she had agreed to spend the summer at the beach. Before she could say anything, David was talking to Ginny.

"I said she *might* be able to spend the summer at the Gull's Nest," he told Ginny mildly. "Actually, Sarah hasn't decided yet—or at least she hadn't last night when I talked to her about it."

"Oh, but you will come, won't you?" Ginny's imploring eyes fastened on Sarah's. "You've got to come. It won't be any fun without you."

"I don't know if I can," Sarah said earnestly to Ginny. "It's almost impossible for me to leave the shop for such a long time. You see . . ."

"Uncle David says you can hire someone to run the shop," Ginny interrupted.

Sarah frowned at David then looked back at Ginny. "That's not all there is to my business," she said gently. "In fact, that's the least of my problems."

"But you can design your clothes at the beach as well as here, can't you?" Ginny asked anxiously. "I mean you don't have to be anywhere special to do that, do you?"

"No, not really, but I do have to talk to my seamstresses frequently to make sure they understand the designs. I need to be on the spot," Sarah said as firmly as she could.

For hours she had been hardening her heart, telling herself she had to resist Ginny's pleas. She hated to disappoint Ginny, but after last night she had no choice. Sarah felt her body grow warm as the events of just a few hours before flashed through her mind. Try though she did, she couldn't forget them. After what had happened, after the things David had said, sharing the same house would be impossible.

Ginny's excitement had evaporated, and she looked so disappointed that Sarah felt her resolve weakening. Though she knew it would be difficult to say no to the little girl, she had not realized it would be quite this difficult.

"You could talk to them on the telephone," Ginny was saying in a trembling voice. "And if there were a real problem, you could drive back to Washington. Bethany Beach is only about three hours away. Uncle David says . . ."

"Your Uncle David says entirely too much," Sarah said sharply.

Instantly she regretted her words, not because of David, but because of Ginny. Ginny had no way of knowing about the undercurrents of emotion which swirled about David and her. The little girl looked confused, and her eyes filled with tears.

"Please come with us," she implored. "We might not be able to go if you don't come."

Sarah winced inwardly. That was hitting below the belt, she thought as she gave David a cold look. He had no right . . . With an inward sigh, she drew Ginny to her.

"I'll see what I can work out," she promised.

Her words were quietly spoken though she was furious with David for putting her in such a position.

He knew very well that she didn't have it in her to spoil Ginny's summer at the beach. No, he wanted Sarah herself at the beach, and he was using Ginny's emotions to get her there. Sarah wasn't exactly sure why he suddenly wanted her at the beach, but after last night, she could make a good guess. That thought made her even more angry.

At her words Ginny brightened immediately. Her eyes began to sparkle with happiness rather than un-shed tears. "We'll have a wonderful time," she pro-claimed. "I just know we will."

She looked first at Sarah, then David as if she expected them to share her happiness.

David, however, was looking aloof, and Sarah was too furious with him to look happy. For Ginny's sake, though she tried. "I'm sure we will."

There was an uncomfortable silence after she spoke. Someone had to say something, and it clearly wasn't going to be David. "Did you call the cottage the Gull's Nest?" Sarah politely asked David.

"Yes," he answered, equally polite. "It has a small widow's walk at the top where the sea gulls like to roost."

Ginny continued to look at the two of them. Her face wore a puzzled look, almost as if she were beginning to sense the underlying tension in the room.

"And you said it's in Bethany Beach?" Sarah said to the little girl. Bethany Beach was a very small town with a reputation for quiet living. It was a family place with a definite and determined lack of night life. Sarah would have expected David's beach house to be in one of the more sophisticated beach communities.

Ginny nodded wordlessly.

"Actually, it's about a mile north of Bethany Beach," David put in.

Ginny suddenly came to life. "I'm going to call my friends and tell them about this summer. They'll be so jealous," she tossed back over her shoulder as she bounded out the rear door of the shop and into Sarah's kitchen.

She left a silence behind her. Again, Sarah was the one to break it. "That was completely unfair," she said to David. Her voice, though accusing, was quiet. She knew it would do her no good to lose her temper.

"Unfair?" he asked. "What was unfair?"

"Telling Ginny she wouldn't be able to go to the beach unless I agreed to go, too."

"I said we *might* not be able to go," he corrected her.

"It was nothing more than emotional blackmail, and you know it," she told him coldly.

He shrugged off her accusation. "Why shouldn't I tell her that? It's true. If you refuse to go, I'll have to hire someone, and that will mean weeks of checking references and investigating backgrounds. In the end, it's very possible we might not be able to go."

"You could spend the summer at the beach yourself," Sarah pointed out. "And then you wouldn't have to hire anyone."

"I've already told you that's impossible. My business requires me to be on the spot."

"So does mine," Sarah said sharply. "Yet you expect me to drop everything simply because you can't be bothered to take some time off." Although Sarah was growing angrier, she kept her voice low. She didn't want Ginny to hear any of their conversation.

"I'm asking you for Ginny's sake." David was suddenly impatient. "Of course I could hire someone to spend the summer at the beach. It's a job a lot of people would jump at. But Ginny wouldn't be happy with just anybody. It's you she loves."

"You're wrong," Sarah said with a cold calm. "She's fond of me, yes. But it's you she loves. You're all the family she has now."

Anger began to shine in David's eyes. "I know that. But I've already told you that I cannot get away for the whole summer."

"So you're shifting your responsibilities to me," Sarah said tiredly. "You know very well that I can't bear to see Ginny hurt—not after everything she's been through. You're taking advantage of that, and of me."

The anger disappeared from his face, and he suddenly sounded indifferent. It was obvious to Sarah that her feelings were of no concern to him.

"I don't understand why there's such a problem. You said yourself that you can design your clothes anywhere. The Gull's Nest has a telephone so you can talk to your staff any time you want to, and you'll be close enough to Washington to handle any emergencies. It seems to me that you're making a mountain out of a molehill."

Sarah just stared at him. She had the feeling she had been very neatly outmaneuvered, and she didn't like it one bit.

"Don't you like Uncle David?" Ginny asked Sarah.

It was late in the morning, and the two of them were finally on their way to the beach.

"Of course I like him," Sarah said cautiously.

She wasn't much in the mood to talk about David. It had been a hectic morning. Leaving her shop in the hands of the woman Sarah had been hurriedly training to be her assistant had been difficult. She knew the woman was completely capable of handling almost anything that might come up, but the thought of leaving her business to someone else was more nerve-wracking than Sarah would have ever believed possible. As she packed the car, she envisioned every possible disaster which could befall her business while she was gone.

By the time she and Ginny were on the way out of the city, Sarah was hot and irritable. Would she even have a business to come back to? she wondered a little despondently.

"What makes you think I don't like him?"

"The way you act," Ginny answered promptly. "You're kind of quiet when he's around."

Sarah studied Ginny's face thoughtfully. She could see it was important to Ginny that she and David like each other. Over the past few weeks, thanks mostly to Sarah's efforts, David and Ginny had drawn a little closer. But their relationship was tenuous at best, and Sarah knew it. The very fragility of their relationship made her sigh with helplessness. Ginny was anxious to love her uncle, but a wrong word could send her back inside herself. As for David, he was trying in a conscientious way to reach out to Ginny, yet Sarah wasn't convinced his heart was in it. His career still came first.

"I don't know him very well," Sarah said finally. She could hardly tell Ginny she found her uncle, despite his faults, wildly attractive. "If I'm more quiet than usual, I suppose that's why. Besides," she reminded the little girl, "it's you he comes to see, not me."

Ginny was not going to be sidetracked. She seemed to sense that Sarah was holding something back. "You'll get to know him better at the beach," she said comfortingly.

"Your uncle may not be able to spend a great deal of time with us this summer," Sarah said, picking her words carefully. "I don't want you to get your hopes up that he'll be there every weekend. His work might keep him in town."

Actually Sarah was sure David would not be spending much time at the beach. He had all but told her that he wouldn't be able to get away often.

"I know he'll come whenever he can," Ginny said blithely.

Sarah sighed but said no more. She was hardly in the mood to discuss David tactfully. As she drove toward the tall, gracefully arched Chesapeake Bay Bridge, however, she felt her spirits lift. All her life she had loved the beach and now, for the first time, she was going to spend the entire summer there.

She counted out her change at the toll booth, then started across the bridge. Beside her, Ginny bounced up and down excitedly as she pointed out sailboats and the huge freighters making their way into the port at Baltimore. Halfway across the bridge Ginny leaned so far out of the car to see what was going on in the water below that Sarah reached across the seat, grabbed her by the waistband of her jeans and hauled her back in.

"What are you trying to do?" she asked. "Swim across? Put your seat belt back on."

Ginny giggled as she pulled the strap across her chest and snapped it into place. "I'm so excited," she said. "How much longer til we get there?"

"Two and a half hours or so."

Sarah couldn't blame her for being excited. She was excited, too. In fact, now that they had left the city behind, she was almost grateful to David for forcing her to take the summer off. Almost, but not quite. Her lips tightened as she remembered the underhanded way he had manipulated and maneuvered her.

That feeling didn't last. Under the influence of the warm, sunny day and Ginny's excitement, it couldn't. A moment later they were across the bridge, and Sarah shrugged away her thoughts. It was too late to worry now. She had the slightly unreal feeling she had left all her cares and responsibilities on the other side of the bay, and she rather liked it. She had nothing to look forward to but sun, sand, relaxing on the beach and . . . David.

Sarah frowned. She didn't want to think about David, but she couldn't help wondering what he would be like away from the businesslike atmosphere of Washington. For a few seconds, she imagined a different David de Courcey. In her mind's eye, she saw him tanned and relaxed by the hot sun, lazing on the beach or in the casual living room of his beach house. In his expressive gray eyes she saw liking . . . no, affection. His smile held a warmth meant only for her.

As they sped down the flat highway, Sarah let her thoughts go farther. She could see the two of them lying on a blanket under the stars, sipping cool wine out of large over-blown wineglasses. She could see the glasses being set aside as David reached for her. She could see him pulling her closer and closer as his lips moved toward hers. For a moment his lips hovered, then brushed hers lightly. He pulled back slightly, smiled tenderly, then kissed her again with a kiss growing in force and passion. Sarah savored his imaginary kiss. She shivered delightedly, and the convulsive movement of her body brought her back to reality.

"Are you all right?" Ginny asked suspiciously. "You've got a funny look on your face. You're not going to be sick or anything, are you?"

Sarah managed to laugh though she felt more embarrassed than she would have if Ginny had actually caught her kissing David. She had been daydreaming like a love struck teenager. "Of course I'm all right. Would you like to stop for some ice cream?" she asked. She had to divert Ginny's attention. She was embarrassed enough by her adolescent daydreams without Ginny asking any more questions.

As she munched on an ice cream cone, Sarah forced herself to put her thoughts into perspective. She couldn't allow her silly fantasies to warp her judgement. In the first place, people didn't change from location to location. David was not going to be any different at the beach than he was in Washington. And in Washington, he was proud, overbearing, used to getting his own way . . . and vulnerable, a small voice suddenly piped up. Sarah ignored it. She had vulnerabilities of her own to deal with.

In the second place, she thought as she tried to discipline her thoughts, his beach house was probably as stiff and formal as he was. Sarah didn't doubt that it would be beautifully furnished but it had very likely been done by a fashionable decorator and was probably more polished than comfortable. It undoubtedly was not the put-your-feet-up kind of place that Sarah saw in her daydreams.

And finally, she told herself firmly, there were not going to be any romantic evenings. The state of affairs between David and her over the past few weeks had been friendly, in a distant, polite sort of way. Sarah knew that was the way things should stay. Anything else would be sheer madness on her part. Oh, she was sure David wouldn't mind a little romantic interlude each time he came to the beach—but for him that was all it would be. A dalliance over the summer to spice up his weekends.

Sarah wasn't made that way. She knew she could never simply walk away from a summer romance. For her it would have to be all or nothing—and, in this case, nothing. She didn't want the summer's legacy to be a broken heart. Sarah sat more stiffly behind the wheel of the car. She didn't like the idea that David had the potential for breaking her heart. She had to keep things between them as they had been during the last few weeks—polite, but nothing more. She had to. She remembered all too well what his touch had done to her that night they had been alone in her house. She remembered, in fact she couldn't forget, how she had lost herself in his kisses.

No, no, no, she thought to herself. That must not happen again. She had to get a hold of herself if the summer was to be at all bearable.

"Is this Bethany Beach?" Ginny asked. She sounded disappointed.

They were driving down the short stretch of town which made up Bethany Beach proper. Sarah laughed. "This is it. It's certainly not very large."

"There's no boardwalk," Ginny wailed. "No rides, no caramel corn, no nothing."

"That's the way they like it," Sarah told her. "The town fathers have deliberately kept the town this way. But don't worry. We'll go to Ocean City or Rehoboth. Both those towns have boardwalks you'll love. Now, let's see if we can find the house."

She left Bethany Beach behind and drove north on the coastal highway. They passed a development of closely spaced beach houses, then came to a stretch where the beach houses were large, airy-looking places with plenty of distance between them. The Gull's Nest had to be in that group, Sarah guessed. David wasn't likely to have a run-of-the-mill place. A moment later she saw a large, three-story house with what appeared to be a picket fence perched on top. That had to be the widow's walk, she thought.

She turned in, and sure enough, a sign said "The Gull's Nest." There was a car parked in front of it, a 1959 Thunderbird. Though the car was old, it had been scrupulously maintained. The light blue paint looked like new, and the dark blue upholstery looked barely worn.

Whose car is it? Sarah wondered. She felt a little uneasy. Surely David wouldn't have offered the use of the house to someone else without telling her. Her unease changed to irritation. Looking after Ginny was one thing, but she had no intention of playing cook and dishwasher to any of David's friends.

Ginny was out of the car as soon as it came to a stop. She sprinted across the dunes toward the beach. Sarah didn't try to stop her. If it hadn't been for the groceries in the back of the car, she would have done the same thing herself. She picked up one of the bags of food and walked up the steps to the door. It was open. She went inside. She was surprised by what she saw. If it hadn't been for the sign, she would have thought she was in the wrong place. The house looked nothing at all like she had imagined. Instead of the trendy, decorator look

Sarah had envisioned, the living room was done in the cooling blues and greens of the ocean. It was a fresh, comfortable atmosphere, and Sarah felt immediately at home.

She stopped staring at the living room and went in search of the kitchen. The groceries were growing heavier by the minute. She pushed open a swinging door with her foot and found herself in an ultra-modern kitchen. The wall overlooking the beach was almost entirely glass and the view was spectacular. Sarah stared around the kitchen in amazement. It was like something out of a magazine. Spending the summer here would certainly be no hardship, she thought dryly. The kitchen was equipped with everything a woman could want. But that was no surprise, Sarah reminded herself. David was used to buying whatever he wanted —be it appliances or people.

She was so engrossed in the kitchen that she didn't notice David until he spoke. When he did, she jumped guiltily. Her thoughts hadn't exactly been charitable.

"Welcome to the Gull's Nest," he said as he came into the kitchen behind her.

Sarah spun around. She was so startled that she almost dropped the groceries. They started to slip, but David caught them before they could fall. As he took the bag from her, his hands brushed hers. He put the groceries on the sparkling counter while Sarah tried to get her thoughts in order.

He was the last person she had expected to find there. If truth be told, he was the last person she *wanted* to find there. As it was, she was completely unprepared for the gamut of emotions she was experiencing—dismay, confusion, delight. "Is that your car?" she asked. It was the first thing that came into her head.

"The T-bird?" He nodded. "Beautiful, isn't it? You know, I always wanted one of those when I was a kid.

When I saw this one for sale a few weeks ago, I couldn't resist it. With that convertible top, it's perfect for the beach."

Sarah stared at him. Her confusion was growing. He was actually smiling at her as if she were someone who mattered. He was talking to her with warmth and enthusiasm in his voice. Gone was the politely distant man who had treated her with such impeccable manners. This David de Courcey was much like the one she had imagined on her way down to Bethany Beach, the one she had told herself could never exist. He was relaxed, charming and friendly.

She studied him as he put the groceries away. He was wearing an open-necked, knit shirt and a pair of very short cut-off jeans bleached a pale blue by the sun. Sarah felt her heart quicken as she looked at him. He looked even better than he did in his expertly cut business suits, if that were possible, she thought to herself. His well-muscled legs were long and tanned, his shoulders were broad. He moved with an ease which hadn't been apparent in Washington. The beach obviously agreed with him.

Sarah's eyes lingered at the casually open neck of his shirt. She could see wisps of dark hair disappearing beneath his shirt, and she felt an unaccountable urge to touch him, to tangle her fingers in the coarse black hair.

Where is Ginny, she wondered frantically. Almost instantaneously she chided herself. It's going to be a long summer, she thought sternly, if she allowed the sight of David in shorts and a knit shirt to affect her like this. What would she do when she saw him in a bathing suit?

"I thought you'd be here sooner," he was saying.

She forced herself to pay attention to his words. No good would come of mooning over his body. "We got a late start," she answered. "I had some things to take care of this morning."

"You look tired," he said. His eyes swept over her critically. His gaze made Sarah feel dusty and unkempt. Although she was wearing crisp white slacks and a fresh-looking, white blouse with small, multi-colored polka dots, she felt wrinkled and considerably worse for wear. She told herself not to be ridiculous. Three hours on the road couldn't possibly have made her look as frowsy as his eyes were making her feel. Annoyed by this sudden urge of hers to look her best for him, she resisted the impulse to pat her hair and make sure her blouse was tucked in. .

"I'm not tired," she started to say.

"Uncle David!" Ginny cried. She had just burst through the door which led from the kitchen to the beach. "What are you doing here? We didn't think you'd come until this weekend."

Ginny stopped a few feet short of her uncle, though Sarah could see from the look in her eyes that she wanted to give him a hug but was half afraid of being rebuffed. Sarah also saw the same impulse in David's eyes, and she saw him check it as Ginny stopped just out of his reach. She felt a pang in her heart, and she forgot her own startled reaction to David's presence as she studied the two of them. They were looking at each other warily; both, it seemed to Sarah, afraid to make the first move, afraid of being hurt.

She sighed. Though they had taken a few steps closer to each other over the past few weeks, it was clear they still had a ways to go. She hoped that by the end of the summer, they would be able to be more spontaneous, more open with each other. Ginny had so much love to give and so did David—whether or not he realized it.

"I was about to ask the same thing," Sarah said to break the silence. "I'm very surprised to find you here."

David gave her an amused glance. She wondered if he had sensed her dismay. "I discovered I could get away so I thought I'd come over and surprise you. You don't mind, do you?"

"Of course we don't," Ginny said happily. "Do we, Sarah?"

David's eyes rested on Sarah's face and in them Sarah could read . . . what? She wasn't quite sure but whatever it was, it was warm and friendly and it made her feel good. Under the influence of that one glance, any misgivings she was suffering disappeared. "No, of course we don't mind," she echoed.

"Good," David said. He gestured around him. "I'm taking care of dinner. All the two of you have to do is relax."

Sarah looked around the kitchen. For the first time she noticed the food on the counters. "I didn't know you could cook," she said. She was amazed. Cooking was one talent she hadn't expected from him.

"Just a few things," he replied modestly. "We're having flounder, locally grown peas and a salad."

"Is that the flounder?" Ginny asked. She pointed at a flat, round fish in the sink. "Did you catch it yourself?"

"I certainly did."

Sarah's amazement grew. This was not the David de Courcey she knew. Ginny, too, seemed surprised. She was looking at her uncle with obvious respect.

"Will you show me how to catch one?" she asked. "I've never been fishing."

"Of course I will. What about you, Sarah?" His eyes lingered warmly on her face. "Are you interested in fishing?"

"Why not?" she said lightly. She couldn't help responding to this new, relaxed David. In Washington he had been distant, stiff and formal. She could scarcely believe the two men were the same person.

"Before we do anything else," he said, "let me show you your rooms. Then I'll carry in your things." He led them up to the second floor, explaining, "There are five bedrooms, but only three of them overlook the ocean. I thought we'd use the ones with the view. Mine is down there."

He gestured toward the end of the hall. Sarah tried not to follow his eyes. She didn't want to know, didn't want to think about his bedroom.

"This one will be yours, Ginny." David showed Ginny the room at the other end of the hall. "And this one will be yours, Sarah." His warm eyes looked into hers for a few breathless seconds before he looked back at Ginny saying, "You can help me bring in the luggage from the car."

As the two of them went down the stairs and out the front door, Sarah leaned back against the wall. The look in David's eyes had left her with a weak feeling she couldn't quite analyze. It was ridiculous, but her knees had actually started to shake and her insides had felt like soft, quivering jelly. She didn't know what to make of this new David. But she did know that he was, if anything, even more attractive and far more dangerous. With the coolly polite David, she could respond in kind. But with this David that would never work. Already it was an effort not to reach out to him—both physically and emotionally. He's too attractive and definitely too charming, she told herself as she went into her bedroom. She *had* to be careful.

Her bedroom was done in white with touches of refreshing ice green. Overlooking the beach were tall French doors leading to a narrow deck. Sarah pushed back the filmy, white cotton curtains and stepped outside. The deck ran the length of the house and was accessible from each of the three bedrooms.

She stepped back into her room, eyeing the cool green coverlet on her bed with approval. The white loveseat across from the bed had pillows of the same green fabric. There were flower prints hanging on the wall and on the dresser stood a beautiful arrangement of white roses, baby's breath and pieces of lush, green fern. She bent over to sniff the flowers.

"Do you like it?" David asked. He came into the room with several pieces of luggage.

"It's lovely," she said, turning around to face him warily.

"I had it made up especially for you." He studied her face intently.

"For me?" she echoed faintly. A light pink color stole into her cheeks. In spite of herself, she couldn't help feeling flattered—though she had no intention of letting him know that. "You needn't have bothered," she said coolly and distinctly.

She didn't want him to think that a bouquet of flowers, no matter how beautiful they were, could make up for the highhanded way he had treated her.

"I want you to be glad you came," he told her. He deposited her luggage by the bed and moved closer. "After all, if I hadn't forced your hand, you probably wouldn't be here." He stopped a few inches away from her.

"You're right," she said in a voice that gave away nothing. "I'd still be in Washington where I belong." There was no reason for him to know how glad she was to be there.

He gave her a rueful glance. "I'm starting to feel a little guilty about the way I treated you." He lifted his hands to her shoulders.

"You should feel guilty." She shrugged his hands away. This new David confused her. She strove to keep her voice noncommittal. "But now that I'm here, I'm sure I'll enjoy myself."

"I hope so," he said softly. He raised his hand and brushed her cheek with his finger. "I want you to enjoy your stay at the Gull's Nest."

He looked down at her and as she stared back into his eyes, it seemed to her that her gaze had gotten tangled up with his. She couldn't pull her eyes away. At that moment Sarah knew that if he took her into his arms, she would go willingly. The thought shocked her. Instinctively she pulled away from him.

David didn't seem to notice. He started to reach out to her and would have said something more, but Ginny burst into the room dragging a suitcase. The moment was lost. David turned away to help her, and Sarah suddenly became aware of the pounding of her heart.

Chapter Five

Sarah didn't know whether to be relieved or annoyed by Ginny's sudden appearance. On reflection, though, she decided she was glad. Things were moving altogether too quickly, and she had to slow them down somehow. She needed time to think over David's new brand of charm before she did something she might later regret.

"How about a swim?" David asked Ginny. "I've got some rafts. We'll blow them up, and I'll show you how to use them to ride the waves."

Ginny squealed. "That sounds like fun. Can we?" She turned questioningly to Sarah.

"I don't see why not," Sarah answered. "Is the water warm enough?"

"It's still on the chilly side, but you'll warm up once you start riding the rafts," David said. "Put your bathing suits on, and I'll meet you downstairs."

Sarah slipped into what had seemed like a fairly

conservative bathing suit in the store where she had bought it. It was white with simple lines which stretched across the contours of her body. It had no straps; instead it fit tightly across her breasts. Sarah had picked it out deliberately. In the store dressing room the suit had seemed the model of decorum. With a high back and an absence of stylish design, Sarah had thought there was nothing about it which would catch David's eye.

Now she wasn't so sure. As she looked in the mirror, it seemed that the suit fit more tightly and outlined the curves of her body more than she remembered. The bodice seemed cut lower too. She tugged at the top, pulling it higher over her bosom. It would have to do, she decided, at least until she could go shopping for another one.

She pulled on a terry cloth cover-up, grateful that she had rejected the white lacy top the saleslady had recommended. Though she had liked the way it looked with the suit, she hadn't wanted anything which would draw David's attention. Her own emotions were hard enough to handle. She didn't want him thinking she was trying to attract him. She had enough to worry about without that.

On the beach, David glanced at her appreciatively as she pulled off her terry shirt but said nothing. Sarah was surprised at how self-conscious she felt under the scrutiny of his eyes, and she resisted the urge to pull her suit up in the front and down in the back. She somewhat crossly reminded herself that she was supposed to possess a degree of sophistication and poise. There was no reason for her to be acting so foolishly simply because she was wearing only a bathing suit.

"Come on in," Ginny shouted. She was bobbing up and down in the water just beyond the point where the waves broke for shore.

Sarah plunged in and moved toward her. The water

felt cold on her body, but as she swam she found it invigorating. A moment later David was beside them with two rubber rafts.

"Climb on," he told Ginny. He passed one raft to Sarah, then helped Ginny to lie down on the other. "Wait until you feel the wave beneath you, then ride it into shore," he told her.

Ginny shook off his hands impatiently, waited for a moment, then let the waves carry her away. She shrieked as the waves took her faster and faster, then pushed her onto the beach.

"Your turn," David said.

Sarah tried to slide onto the raft but couldn't. The water was over her head and every time she tried to get on, she slid right back off again. David, who seemed to be having no trouble as the water ebbed and swelled, put his hands around her waist and lifted her effortlessly onto the raft. Sarah felt a shock as his hands closed around her waist, but that was nothing to what she felt when he patted her bottom.

"Go to it," he said, laughing.

Before she could glare at him, a wave caught her raft. Sarah rode it about two feet before she tipped over and sank to the bottom. She floundered for a moment, then David's hands brought her back to the surface.

"Are you all right?" he asked. His voice contained the right amount of concern, but his eyes were laughing.

Sarah pushed him away a little crossly. She was embarrassed that she couldn't do what Ginny had done so effortlessly. She was also annoyed with herself for wanting to cling to him in the water. His body seemed to be the one firm place in the swirling ocean.

"Try again," he said.

Once more he helped her on the raft, and again Sarah waited until she felt the wave swell beneath her. She got a little farther this time but she still wasn't able to ride the wave all the way to the beach. Instead she was unceremoniously dumped before she had gone too far. David pulled her back to the surface, and this time Sarah wasn't so quick to push him away. Instead she let his hands support her as she caught her breath. She could feel the warmth of his fingers just below her breasts.

Ginny bobbed up beside her. "You've got to balance yourself," she advised.

"It's just like riding a bicycle," David told her. He was grinning openly. "Your body has to move with the raft, not against it."

"Watch me," Ginny called. She jumped onto her raft, then was off. "It's easy," her voice floated back to Sarah.

"Do you want to try one more time?" David asked.

Sarah pushed back a strand of wet hair. "Of course I do," she said, though she really didn't. Her pride wouldn't let her quit after only two tries. With a sigh of resignation, she got back on the raft and waited. A moment later, David pushed her off, and she concentrated on balancing. She was just beginning to feel she had done it when the wave she was riding broke and turned her head over heels. The water pushed her down to the floor of the ocean where the undertow caught her and scraped her along the pebble-filled bottom. She was beginning to panic when David's hands again came to her rescue. He pulled her out of the water and held her close to him. The laughter had disappeared from his eyes, and he stroked her back as she clung to him, gasping for air.

"It's all right," he said soothingly, as though he were talking to a child. "I've got you. You're safe."

Sarah put her arms around his neck and let him press her against him. She was trembling with fright. "The water," she said gasping for air. "I couldn't breathe."

"I know," he said comfortingly. "You have to relax

when you get caught by the undertow. It will let you go. It's not really very strong here, you know. But if you fight it, it's worse."

Sarah nodded though she wasn't paying too much attention to his words. She was still breathing quickly, but it was no longer because of fright. The heat of David's bare chest was burning through her thin bathing suit. Though she knew she should release him, though she knew she had to let him go, she clung to him nonetheless.

He scooped her into his arms and carried her out of the water and onto the beach. Gently, he put her down and began drying her with a towel. Ginny hovered over her so anxiously that Sarah began to feel foolish. David used the towel to pat her shoulders, her neck, her chest. Sarah looked down and saw that her bathing suit had slipped several inches. She blushed, pulled it up, and vowed that her next one would have straps. "I'm all right," she said, pushing David's hands away. "After all, nothing really happened."

"You gave us quite a scare," David said. He sat back on his heels and looked at her.

"I'll say," Ginny said. "I thought you were never going to come up." Her eyes grew round. "I'll bet Uncle David saved your life."

There was a gleam in David's eyes. "Isn't there an old custom that if a person saves a life, the life he saves becomes his to do with as he pleases?"

"There is," Ginny cried. "We talked about it once in school. You belong to Uncle David now," Ginny said to Sarah. "You have to do whatever he says. What are you going to do with her?" she asked her uncle.

David's eyes were fixed speculatively on Sarah's face. She blushed as she looked into them. She knew very well what he would like to do with her.

"I don't know," David said. "I'll think of something." His eyes swept Sarah's face, noting the color in her cheeks. "I'll think of something," he repeated softly.

"Why don't you two go back in the water," Sarah managed to say.

The unmistakable look in David's eyes was making her throat feel tight and her breath come unevenly. She reached for the towel and wrapped it around her shoulders as though it would offer her some protection against the desire in his eyes . . . desire which her own body was starting to match.

"I'll watch you from here," she added firmly.

"Are you sure you're all right?" David asked. His large hands smoothed the towel over her shoulders and settled it into place across her chest.

"Of course I am," she answered quickly. She wanted to push him away, but Ginny's presence stopped her. In Ginny's eyes, David was now a hero and, as a hero, deserved to be treated at least politely. Sarah could imagine the look on Ginny's face if she jerked away from David or told him to keep his hands to himself. Unfortunately, that was just what she wanted to do. His touch, even through the thick terry cloth, was almost unbearable to Sarah. His hands moved slowly and lazily as he made sure she was dry. She began to tremble, more from the effect of his contact with her body than anything else.

"You're cold," he said suddenly. "I can feel you trembling."

"No, I'm not," she started to say. She changed her mind midway through the sentence. "Perhaps I am a little cold." She scrambled to her feet, refusing to meet David's eyes. "I think I'll go in and take a hot shower."

She knew he was looking at her quizzically. She couldn't look him in the face for fear he'd see the panic in her eyes. She wanted desperately to get away from him, but she didn't want him to see how great her desperation was. She couldn't let him know how undone she was by his touch.

"Do you want us to go in with you?" Ginny asked, though it was obvious from the look on her face that she didn't want to.

Sarah gave her a quick hug. "Don't be silly. You and your uncle stay here and enjoy yourselves." Still without meeting David's eyes, she turned and took a few steps toward the house. She could feel him staring after her. It wasn't until she heard their footsteps on the sand that she turned to watch them. As she watched, they ran into the water and dove under the waves. At any other time, she would have been delighted with the camaraderie they were displaying. But now, Sarah was preoccupied. She felt drained by the buffeting she had received from the waves and her own physical reaction to David's touch.

"Dinner's ready," David called.

Sarah was upstairs, unpacking clothes. She had left Ginny and David alone in the kitchen partly because they seemed to be having such a good time together that she hated to interrupt, and partly because she needed time away from David. She had to get her feelings under control.

"I made the salad," Ginny announced proudly as Sarah sat down on one of the white, lacquered chairs in the dining room.

The dining room, like the kitchen, overlooked the beach. From her chair, she could see that the moon was just beginning to rise over the water. It faintly illuminated the empty beach.

"I also set the table," Ginny said as she carefully lit the candles she had put out. Each candle, each plate and each napkin was a different color. "Isn't it pretty?"

"It's lovely," Sarah assured her.

"Not to mention colorful," David put in.

Ginny took that as a compliment. "It's just like those table settings we saw at Bloomingdale's," she said with satisfaction.

"You haven't seen the third floor of the house yet, have you?" David asked as they ate the flounder he had sautéed. It was topped with a parsleyed butter sauce.

"I didn't know there was one," Ginny said. "Did you?" she asked Sarah.

Sarah shook her head. "I noticed the stairs but I thought they led to an attic."

"What's up there?" Ginny wanted to know.

"Just a television and a stereo," he told her. "You can see it after we've done the dishes."

Ginny groaned.

Just a television indeed, Sarah thought later as she surveyed the large, third-story room. It was more like a video center. The television, at one end of the room, was a large, wide-screened projection model which seemed ideal for showing movies. There was also a very elaborate stereo system and a smaller television which served as the screen for an assortment of video games. A long, comfortable sofa covered in a nubby, cotton fabric and several overstuffed chairs were the room's only furniture. French doors led to a small balcony overlooking the beach.

"You've got everything here but a computer," Sarah said in awe.

"That's downstairs in the study," he said. "I use it when I work here."

He turned and caught the look on her face. As usual, he seemed to read her thoughts. He smiled a little sheepishly. "I know what you're thinking. But I don't get much time to relax and when I do, I want everything at my fingertips."

"Where do those stairs lead?" she asked, pointing to the circular staircase in one corner of the room.

"They go up to the widow's walk. Would you like to see it?"

Sarah glanced over at Ginny. She was sitting on the floor in front of the smaller television, completely absorbed in one of her uncle's video games.

David followed Sarah's glance. "She won't even miss us," he said. "Come on. I'll show it to you."

Sarah followed him up the narrow steps until she climbed out onto a small square enclosed by a waist-high fence. It was easily the tallest point around. Above them the sky had darkened, and the stars were shining brightly. A small slice of moon spotlighted the waves of the ocean. Sarah was suddenly very conscious of David standing close.

"What do you think of the Gull's Nest?" he asked quietly.

It didn't sound like an idle question. Sarah had the feeling he really wanted to know. "It's fantastic," she said simply. "I've never seen anything like it, never even imagined anything like it."

"But do you like it?" he persisted.

"Very much," she answered softly.

He seemed to relax slightly, and Sarah wondered why it was so important to him that she like it.

"So do I," he told her. "When I'm here I feel like a different person."

And you act like one, too, Sarah thought, though she didn't say it. She didn't want to say anything that would upset the feeling that seemed to be growing around them. David gently cupped her face with his hand and raised it so he could look at her. Sarah stared back at him, mesmerized by the gentleness in his eyes.

"I want you to be happy here," he told her. "Very happy." His voice was low and thrilling. Sarah's heart began to pound.

He lowered his lips to hers and kissed her tenderly. Sarah felt her bones dissolve at his touch. He lifted his head slightly as his hands slid from her face to her neck and caught at her shoulders. They gazed at each other wordlessly. Something was happening between them, something both frightening and exhilarating. Sarah felt a yearning in her body which was more than physical desire and which she instinctively knew was matched in

David's body. Their eyes locked together, he began to pull her toward him. Sarah moved closer, unable to look anywhere but into the deep stillness of his eyes. As she stepped into the protective circle of his arms, she had the feeling she was coming home. She trustingly raised her lips to his, only to have the world return with a clatter.

"Hey, you guys," Ginny called. "What are you doing up there?" She pushed open the door and looked around her with undisguised pleasure. "This is great," she exclaimed. "In the daytime, I'll bet you can see Europe."

"Perhaps not quite that far," David said dryly. "But you can see quite a ways."

Sarah was speechless. For a few moments she and David had spun a web of magic around themselves. Now it was gone and she was feeling a little bereft. She looked over at David and saw that he was watching her intently. Then she dropped her gaze. She had already shown him far too much.

Silently she followed Ginny down the stairs. There, the outward part of her moved a space warrior around the blank television screen while the inner part of her mulled over what had happened up on the widow's walk.

The next morning, Sarah walked north on the nearly deserted beach, hugging her sweater to her. It was quite early and, aside from a few fishermen, she was alone. The fishermen didn't really count, she decided as she stayed high on the beach to avoid walking into their fishing lines. Like her, they were enjoying the solitude of the cool hours of early morning. Like her, they had no desire to start a conversation. A few nodded politely, but most stared at the hypnotic motion of the waves.

Sarah kicked at the sand as she walked. Now and then she picked up an interesting seashell. Mostly, though, she thought about David. Twice yesterday Ginny had interrupted moments which had promised to develop into something very special. If, as it was said, the eyes were the mirror to one's soul, Sarah knew that last night on the widow's walk she had let David see things which would be better kept to herself. She had let him see just how attracted she was to him. That wasn't the worst of it, she thought with a sigh. He already knew that. It was impossible to keep such knowledge from a man like David de Courcey.

What upset her most was the fact that she had let him see the yearning, the longing she felt for a meeting of their minds and bodies. She had let down her guard, given too much of herself away. At the time, she had thought she saw feelings which matched hers reflected in his eyes. Now, she wasn't so sure. Casual affairs were undoubtedly commonplace to David. Perhaps that soul-stirring look was merely part of his technique, Sarah told herself. The magic she had felt growing up around them had undoubtedly existed only in her mind.

Sarah had left the house early so she wouldn't run into David before she had her thoughts in order. She had felt shy at the prospect of seeing him again. But now she thought she knew the best way to treat him. She would be friendly—Ginny would notice if she weren't—but slightly standoffish. David would get the message.

"Sarah!" David's familiar voice broke the early morning stillness. Sarah had been so engrossed in her own thoughts that she had nearly walked by him. As she heard his voice, she felt a leap of pleasure deep inside her. She walked toward him with both reluctance and anticipation. With each step, she reminded herself of the new attitude she was going to display.

"What brought you out so early?" he asked. He gave her an engaging grin which made Sarah's heart flutter.

"I like the early morning when there aren't many people about," Sarah said a little lamely. She could hardly tell him she had gone for a walk to avoid meeting him until she knew where she stood. "Have you caught anything?"

He gestured toward a bucket of water. In it was a fairly good-sized bluefish.

"Tonight's dinner," he told her. He lifted his pole from the sand and expertly cast the line into the water. Sarah watched as it effortlessly sailed across the waves and sank into the water.

"I caught it just before I saw you." His line gave an almost imperceptible jerk. "I think I've got another one. There must be a school of them out there." He gave the fish a little line, then began reeling it in. A moment later, he had the fish off the hook and in the pail beside him.

"Do you want to try it?" he asked as he cut up a piece of shrimp and baited the hook.

Sarah took a step backward. "No, thanks. I don't know anything about casting."

"It's easy. I'll show you how. Come on over here." Again he gave her that engaging grin of his, and before she realized she had moved, Sarah was standing beside him. He handed her the pole and Sarah took it gingerly. Putting his arms around her, he helped her flip the hook over the waves and into the water. Sarah stood where she was, not moving, barely even breathing. She had forgotten the fishing pole in her hands, forgotten why she was standing in David's arms. All she cared about was the contact of her body and his. She felt a warm glow spreading over her. Bemused, she leaned back slightly against him.

David responded by brushing away her hair and kissing her neck. The touch of his lips sent chills down Sarah's back. She was hoping he would kiss her again when a man's voice broke through her reverie.

"Caught anything?" It seemed to be the universal greeting among fishermen.

"Two blues," David said. He stepped away from

Sarah, leaving her with the fishing pole and a feeling of annoyance toward the man who had intruded on their privacy.

While the other man set up his line, he and David talked bait and fishing conditions. Sarah stood by silently. She was beginning to feel a little silly. For one thing, she had no idea what she was supposed to be doing with the fishing pole in her hands. For another thing, she had wanted to avoid David. Instead of showing him she was not interested in letting their relationship grow more intimate, she had allowed herself to be led into his arms like a lamb to the slaughter. And she had actually shivered with delight at the touch of his lips on her bare neck.

"I think I've got something," she said suddenly. There was excitement in her voice. The line had gone taut and even she, inexperienced as she was, could feel the pull of something at the other end. "What do I do?" she asked urgently.

Instantly David's arms were around her again. This time, though, both of them concentrated on the fish.

"I think it's a big one," David said.

"You bring it in by yourself," Sarah said. She tried to step out of the circle of his arms.

"No," he said crisply. "We'll bring it in together. Just do what I tell you."

With David's arms around her, steadying her, giving her support, Sarah let out the line, playing with the fish for a few minutes until it tired itself out. Then she slowly reeled it in. As she stood there, intent on bringing in the fish, her excitement grew.

"What if it gets away?" she asked nervously.

"It won't," David said calmly. "Just bring it in slowly.

Sarah did as she was told and when the fish, a sea trout, was lying at her feet, she dropped the pole, turned, flung her arms around David and hugged him tightly.

"We did it!" she cried triumphantly.

"You did it," David corrected her. "All I did was to help you a little." He held her to him for a second then released her. Sarah looked into his eyes and felt her heart turn over. If only they were alone, she thought. David dropped a kiss on the top of her head as the other man knelt to examine the fish.

"Good job," he exclaimed. "She's a beauty."

David knelt down beside him and removed the hook from the fish's mouth.

"You should take it down to the marina," the fisherman said. "They have a weekly big fish contest. You might win."

"I'll do that," David said.

"It's not that big, is it?" Sarah asked. To her it looked huge, but she thought that was probably just because she wasn't used to fish.

"It's about ten pounds," the man answered. "That's pretty big for this time of year. I remember once . . ."

He embarked on a long, involved fishing story while Sarah stood by impatiently wishing he would leave. She wanted to be alone with David. It wasn't until the man had actually cast his line into the water that she faced the fact that he was there to stay.

"I think I'll go in and fix some fruit for breakfast," she said when the man had finally finished his interminable story.

"Bacon and eggs for me," David said. "I'll be up in a half hour or so. I want to see if I can match your catch." He lightly touched her cheek then turned his attention to the fishing.

Sarah dreamily made her way back to the house. She knew she had ignored her early morning resolution to keep David in his place. Strangely enough, she didn't care.

The day rushed by. After breakfast, Ginny and David drove off in the light blue Thunderbird to enter her fish in the big catch contest. Sarah slid into her bathing suit and went out to sunbathe. She tried to read, but she was too happy to concentrate. Eventually the warm rays of the sun relaxed her and she fell asleep. She awoke to feel David's hands spreading a sunscreen on her back and shoulders.

"You should be careful," he said when he saw that she was awake. Though his eyes were warm, his voice was reproving. "With this creamy white skin of yours, you'll burn easily."

"I meant to put some on, but I forgot," Sarah said. She lay on her stomach, enjoying the feel of David's fingers stroking on the cool, silky lotion. His hands moved slowly over her back and shoulders in a caress that was more sensual than medicinal.

He squirted more of the lotion on his hands then began stroking it onto her legs. Sarah repressed a gasp as he touched the back of her thigh. Lazily he worked the lotion into her skin. Slowly his hand traveled from her thigh down to the calf of her leg. By the time he moved to the other leg, there was a tension in the air, and Sarah felt as if her insides had dissolved. Her legs were too heavy to move. All she could do was lie there and enjoy the sensation of his hands smoothing on the sunscreen.

"Roll over," he said. "I'll do the other side." His voice was thick with emotion.

Sarah rolled over. She looked at him for one long, paralyzing moment before she found her voice.

"I'll do it," she said a little unsteadily. She didn't want him to go on touching her. Or did she? She stretched out her hand for the bottle of lotion. David held on to it as his eyes searched hers. The look on his face brought a pale pink to her cheeks. What was he looking for?

"Here I come," Ginny called as she ran across the beach to where they were sitting.

Wordlessly, David gave Sarah the bottle. She took it and bent her head. She didn't want to see the look in his eyes any longer. His desire, for that was what she had seen, had too profound an affect on her.

"Let's go in the water, Uncle David," Ginny cried as she dropped her things beside Sarah. He got to his feet. "Want to come?" she asked Sarah.

"A little later," Sarah told her. With a feeling akin to relief, she watched the two of them plunge into the water.

"What will we do tomorrow?" Ginny asked as she brushed her hair. Dinner was over, the dishes were done, and she was getting ready for bed.

"I don't know," Sarah replied. "What would you like to do?"

"Go to Rehoboth and see the boardwalk," Ginny told her promptly. "Do you think Uncle David will take us?"

"You'll have to ask him and see . . . tomorrow," Sarah said as Ginny made a bee-line for the door. "Not now. He's in his study catching up on a little work. Anyway, it's time for you to be in bed."

Ginny groaned but climbed in bed anyway. "I'm glad we came," she said as she snuggled down under the lightweight covers. "Aren't you?"

"Yes, I am," Sarah told her softly. She leaned over and kissed Ginny good night. "I'm going upstairs to read and listen to a little music before I go to bed. Call if you need me."

"Okay." Ginny's eyelids were already beginning to close.

"Sweet dreams." Sarah tiptoed out of the room.

Upstairs, she put Chopin on the stereo, kicked off her sandals and curled up on the deep, plush sofa. She was wearing a long white caftan made of thin, cotton material. The wrist-length sleeves and the open neck of the caftan were trimmed with a delicate, mid-ocean blue embroidery.

Sarah leaned back and opened her book, a biography

of Coco Chanel. She was hoping it would take her mind off David. For a while it worked. She was deep in the early years of Chanel's life when she became aware of the salt-laden evening breeze filling the room. She looked up to see David opening the French doors to the small balcony.

"I thought you had work to do," Sarah said a little nervously.

"I've finished," he told her. "For the time being, at least."

"I came up here to be out of your way," she told him uneasily. She meant that though it was more for her own sake than his, that she wanted to be out of his way.

"That wasn't necessary. Besides, you'd never be in my way." His eyes were warm, giving his words a special meaning.

Sarah closed her book hastily. "I think I'll go to bed." She knew retreat would be the wisest course of action. Standing across the room, looking devastatingly handsome in his white slacks and open-necked sports shirt, he couldn't know he was making her heart beat faster. Sarah knew it though. She felt the increased tempo and, along with it, a growing desire to slip her arms around his neck and pull his face down to hers so she could caress his lips.

Dismayed, she started to get to her feet. She had to get away from David, and quickly. She was too vulnerable to his attentions to risk staying. Every time he had touched her that day, she had realized that.

"Don't go," he said, crossing the room and sitting down beside her. "I thought we could talk."

Sarah sank back into the corner of the sofa. She was at war with herself. A part of her, the sensible part, wanted her to get up at once and leave the room. The other part of her, the part she usually kept suppressed, the romantic part, urged her to stay. He smiled engagingly and the romantic part of her won. She leaned back and gave him a tremulous smile in return. At the same time, she felt her guard go up. He was dangerous and she would be wise to remember it.

"Ginny seems to be having a good time," he said. "I think she's finding out I'm not so bad after all. She doesn't think the worst of me anymore."

"She never thought the worst of you," Sarah told him. She wanted him to know just how much Ginny cared. "It's simply that she's been afraid to show you how much she cares for you."

"What about you?" he asked lightly. "Are you finding out I'm not as bad as you had thought?"

Sarah looked at him in some confusion. Was he teasing? "Well," she said hesitatingly. "You do seem to be a different person here at the beach."

His smile broadened. "Does that mean you like the Gull's-Nest me, but you don't like the Washington me?"

"That's not what I mean at all," Sarah protested even though there was quite a bit of truth to his words. She did like this David very much. The other David de Courcey was a cool, infuriating man who annoyed her more than anything else.

She saw a gleam in his eye and realized he was teasing her. It probably hadn't seriously occurred to him that there might be some aspect of his personality she didn't like. He was too used to the adulation of Washington's most glamourous women. Because of that, his self-confidence knew no limits.

"How long are you thinking of staying?" Sarah asked.

"At least through the weekend," he told her. "And perhaps the early part of next week as well."

Sarah felt her spirits shoot absurdly high, but she immediately repressed her excitement. It was ridiculous to think that the prospect of seeing him for several more days could make her so happy. "That's wonderful," she said sedately. "Ginny will be delighted."

"I hope you're delighted, too." He picked up her

hand and entwined her fingers with his. He seemed to be expecting an answer, but Sarah's mouth was suddenly dry and she was unable to speak.

"It's hard to get you alone," he said, as his other hand slid over the back of the sofa and rested on her neck. "Ginny has a way of appearing at the most inopportune times." His fingers traced a pattern around her neck and came to a stop under her chin. He leaned over and kissed the tender skin below her ear. As his lips moved forward, Sarah let her head fall back on the sofa. His lips continued to nibble at her neck until she shivered. Then he cradled the back of her head in his hand and brought it toward him.

Sarah gazed with helpless longing into his eyes. She knew what was coming. She welcomed it. And yet . . . in the farthest corners of her mind a small voice warned her to be careful. Sarah ignored it. She couldn't have pushed him away now if she wanted to. Her body was suddenly powerless. Besides, she didn't want to push him away. She wanted to pull him closer.

His lips pressed against hers gently, then with more intensity. Sarah suddenly found herself lying across his lap with her arms wrapped around his neck. He pulled away slightly and gave her a lazy smile. Sarah tried to smile back but she couldn't. Her lips ached to be kissed again and again.

David must have seen the impatience in her eyes, because he drew her to him. Sarah went eagerly, wriggling in his arms as she tried to get closer and closer. David's lips found hers. This time Sarah could feel the warmth of his tongue as it probed insistently. Her heart felt as if it would slam against her rib cage, and she let her lips part slightly in response.

As David invaded her mouth, his hands began caressing her body. They moved down her back and over her thighs. His hand came to a halt on the satiny soft skin of Sarah's upper thigh. As she had pressed herself against him, her dress had ridden up, leaving her legs bare as they stretched out on the sofa. Sarah went limp as his hand began a languorous movement over her legs. Desire coursed through her, a desire so strong that it wiped all thought from her mind.

Slowly, with no hint of impatience, David shifted her body slightly so that he could loosen the tangle her dress had made beneath her. When the dress was no longer stretched tightly over her body, his hand slipped underneath it and upward. Sarah gasped with pleasure as his hand moved across her stomach. When he touched her breast, she began to tremble.

Her trembling was caused in part by the wild longing which was growing stronger with each passing moment. It was also caused by fear. Everything was moving just a little too quickly. Her common sense cried out to her to stop what they were doing before it was too late. No matter how frightened she was, though, she wasn't sure she could stop what was happening. These sensations were more than she had bargained for. They were stronger, more powerful than anything she had ever imagined. Still, she knew she had to try.

"Aren't you being a little hypocritical?" she asked, trying to keep her voice light. She didn't want to make him angry, not now that a kind of rapport seemed to be growing up between them, but she didn't want him to get the idea that she was his for the asking, either.

He raised his head and gave her a bewildered glance. "Hypocritical?" His voice was hoarse.

"A few weeks ago you were very concerned about what went on while Ginny was sleeping. I seem to recall you lecturing me about my morals." Sarah's voice lost some of its lightness. Just the thought of that evening made her angry.

David's eyes darkened. "That was different. What Ginny doesn't know won't hurt her . . . and there's no reason for her to know about this." His lips slid across her neck and down the slit in her dress.

Sarah's mind followed his lips down her body, and

for a moment the feelings they produced threatened to overcome the anger which was welling up inside her. "You *are* a hypocrite!" she said accusingly. Her voice was unsteady.

David tilted her head back. "Look at me," he commanded.

Reluctantly, Sarah looked up. Her eyes showed him all the emotions she was feeling . . . confusion, fear, anger and desire.

Something flickered in the back of his eyes. "I may be a hypocrite," he said hoarsely, "but at the moment, I don't care." His mouth closed over hers with a possessive urgency which set this kiss apart from all the others.

A darkness overtook Sarah. She no longer saw the lights in the room; she no longer heard the ocean lapping gently at the shore or Chopin on the stereo. Her anger disappeared. Everything disappeared. Only David existed. She saw nothing, heard nothing but . . .

"Sarah!"

Somewhere in the world beyond them, a voice was calling out to her. She heard it again.

"Sarah!"

It was Ginny and she sounded frightened.

David lifted his head. "Damn," he said softly.

Sarah could hear the frustration in his voice. She knew just how he felt. She swung her legs to the floor, wondering if she would be able to walk to the door and down the stairs. Waves of desire were still flooding over her, and her knees felt weak, too weak to carry her far.

"Sarah!" came Ginny's voice a third time.

Without a word, she crossed the room and hurried down the steps. She was beginning to feel a little embarrassed by what had just taken place. "What is it, honey?" she asked as she entered Ginny's room. Her voice sounded as though she had been running, but she couldn't help that.

Ginny was sitting up in bed crying. "I had a bad

dream," she said. "There was something coming in the window, and it got all over my face. I couldn't get away from it."

Sarah looked at the window beside Ginny's bed. "It was just the moonlight shining in," she said soothingly. "Somehow your mind caught hold of it and turned it into a nightmare."

"Do you really think that's what it was?" Ginny asked. Her tears had stopped now that Sarah was sitting beside her.

"Of course. What else could it have been?"

"A monster," Ginny said sleepily. She slid back down on the bed. "Will you close the curtains for me?"

Sarah closed the curtains.

"And stay with me until I go back to sleep?"

"Of course I will," Sarah said.

Ginny's hand stole into hers and Sarah sat on the side of the little girl's bed until she could tell by her breathing that Ginny was again asleep. As Sarah sat there, she tried not to think of David upstairs . . . waiting for her.

She sat in the darkness of Ginny's room for a few minutes while she tried to get hold of herself. Nervously she pressed her hands to her hot face. What should she do? If she went back upstairs, David would want to pick up where they had left off. So would she, for that matter. And Sarah knew where that would lead. Her common sense began making itself heard, and now Sarah listened to it. She wasn't ready for what would happen if she went back to David. She would probably never be ready to be part of a summer love affair.

Sarah forced herself to face the truth even though it hurt. David wasn't interested in anything but a summer romance, if you could call the sexual electricity between them romance, she told herself wryly. And that didn't interest her in the least. Away from the force of his personality and the magic of his kisses, she could see that.

Quietly she left Ginny's room. In the hall she forced herself to turn toward her bedroom, not the stairs. A part of her still urged her to go back to David, to finish what they had started. It was what she really wanted, that part of her said. Sarah didn't listen. Instead she listened to her common sense. She was not going to let David hurt her, and he would if she allowed herself to be treated as a summer convenience—one of the amenities of the Gull's Nest.

Resolutely Sarah went into her room and closed the door behind her. Without thinking of David, she slipped on her nightgown. As she turned off the light, there was a creak on the stairs. In the dark, her hearing seemed unusually acute. She heard David walk softly down the hall and peek into Ginny's room. Then she heard his footsteps coming closer to her own room. She froze. What if he came in?

He stopped just outside her door and knocked lightly. "Sarah?" he called softly. The sound of his voice was almost her undoing.

"David," she tried to say, but her voice didn't make a sound.

He didn't wait long enough for her to say his name again. She heard him move down the hall to his own room, heard the door to his room close decisively. She lay on the bed miserably, wondering whether it was Ginny or her own doubts which had saved her.

Chapter Six

Sarah was in the kitchen fixing breakfast for Ginny when David entered the room. With her back to the door, she heard rather than saw him come in. She didn't turn around, choosing instead to concentrate on the eggs she was scrambling. As she felt his presence in the room, a warmth which had nothing to do with the heat from the stove crept into her cheeks. Sarah dreaded facing him. After last night, she hated the thought of what might be in his eyes.

"Why are you all dressed up?" Ginny asked suspiciously.

Sarah finished spooning eggs onto a plate and forced herself to turn around. She had to face him sooner or later. Her eyes widened with surprise. David was wearing a light gray summer suit with a loosely knotted tie around his neck.

"Good morning," he said in even tones as she turned.

"Would you like some breakfast?" she asked.

"Just orange juice," he told her impersonally.

With a hand not quite steady, Sarah poured the orange juice. She needn't have worried about what she'd see in his eyes, she told herself. There was nothing to see—no warmth, no friendliness. There was just a chilly politeness.

"Why are you all dressed up?" Ginny asked again. Her voice was plaintive.

Sarah put David's orange juice on the table in front of him. He picked it up and sipped it as he stood there. "I've got to go back to Washington," he said.

"But I thought you'd stay through the weekend at least," Ginny wailed.

"Something came up," he said. "I've got to get back to the office."

"When will you be back?"

"I don't know. I'll have to call you and let you know."

"I wanted you to take us to Rehoboth today," Ginny said unhappily. "To see the boardwalk."

Sarah put her hands on Ginny's shoulders. "We'll go without your uncle." Over Ginny's head, she gave him a measured look. Couldn't he see how unhappy he was making her? He returned her look with one of his own that yielded nothing.

"Will you walk out to the car with me?" he asked Sarah. "There's something I want to talk to you about."

"Of course," Sarah said in a tone which matched his in polite impersonality. What was wrong, she was wondering frantically. Where was the friendliness, the camaraderie of yesterday?

She had only been half-kidding when she told herself there were two Davids, but it certainly seemed that once he put on a suit, he became more annoying, harder to understand.

"Eat your breakfast," Sarah said to Ginny as she crossed the room to the door which David was holding open. "We'll go out after we do the dishes and make the beds."

She and David walked through the house in silence. With each step, Sarah was growing angrier. She waited until she was sure Ginny couldn't overhear her before she spoke.

"Can't you see how unhappy you're making Ginny?" she said as they stepped outside. "Why are you leaving, anyway?"

"I told you, something came up," he replied crisply. "That's not what I want to talk about. What happened to you last night?"

"What happened to me?" Sarah echoed uncomfortably. That was something she didn't want to talk about. She was too embarrassed by the way she had behaved to talk about it.

"I waited for you to come back upstairs. What made you change your mind?"

Sarah glanced briefly, very briefly, into his eyes. He was angry, and she couldn't blame him. Nothing in her behavior had given him any indication that she would run from him at practically the last minute.

She took a deep breath and decided to be honest with him—as honest as she could be. "Things were moving a little too quickly," she told him with as much confidence as she could muster. "I haven't . . . I'm not . . . I just wasn't ready," she finished lamely.

"You were plenty ready before Ginny interrupted us," he told her roughly. "What made you change your mind?"

Sarah shook her head helplessly. She didn't know what had made her change her mind. And she wasn't sure she could tell him about it, even if she knew. Not in his present mood. Yesterday, when he had been warm and friendly, she might have been able to talk to him. But talking to this cold, demanding stranger was simply not possible.

"Don't you think you could at least have told me of

your change of heart before you ran off to your room?"
he asked sarcastically.

Sarah flushed at the tone of his voice and his words.
She had run off to her room and she knew it. She just
hoped he didn't realize how desperate, and how difficult to make, her flight had been.

"I didn't think you'd understand." It was not a very
good excuse but it was the best she could do. She simply
could not tell him how much she had wanted to go back
to his arms or how terrified she was of being hurt. A
summer romance for him was probably an annual
event, for her it could be devastating. That was something he would never be able to understand.

"You didn't think I'd understand," he repeated with
a dangerous softness. "What did you think, then? That
I'd force you to make love to me? Is that what you
thought?"

He sounded even angrier than before, though Sarah
wasn't quite sure why. She did know one thing. If she
had gone back upstairs last night, no force would have
been necessary. She had wanted him as much as he had
wanted her, but she was not going to allow herself to
become his summer fling. How could she explain that
to him? she asked herself.

She couldn't. He was too angry, too used to getting
his own way, and she was too unnerved to even begin
such an explanation. Suddenly a light shone in her
mind. "Is that why you're leaving?" she asked incredulously. "Because I went to my room instead of back
upstairs?" That made sense. Only last night he had said
that he would be staying until the early part of next
week. A problem at the office was nothing more than
an excuse to get away. What could possibly have
cropped up during the middle of the night?

"Is that why you're leaving?" Her tone demanded an
answer.

He gave her a withering look. "Don't flatter yourself."

Sarah was suddenly furious. There was no reason why she had to stand there defending herself. Her decisions were her own, and she didn't have to explain them to him, or to anyone.

"If you're punishing Ginny because you're angry with me, you're being very childish," she said in a low, controlled voice.

He turned the ignition key and the car began to purr. "I'm leaving because my presence is required at the office," he said coldly. "You're the one who is childish if you think my coming and going has anything to do with you."

That was precisely the problem, Sarah thought to herself. That was why she had to keep her distance. His coming and going had nothing to do with her. To him, she was just a convenience, like the dishwasher or the washing machine. Well, she would put a stop to that.

"Before you go," she began, "I want you to understand one thing. I don't have to justify my behavior to you in any way. If I chose not to sleep with you, that's my business. I'm not here to entertain you whenever you decide to come to the beach. I'm not your summer plaything, and I refuse to be treated like one. And," she finished up, "I'm not going to make love to you simply because we are staying under the same roof. Is that clear?"

His angry eyes met hers. "You've made yourself perfectly clear. Now, if you'll excuse me, I have to be going."

Sarah stepped away from the car. He roared down the driveway, leaving a cloud of swirling sand behind him. She turned and stalked into the house. Who does he think he is, she stormed as she climbed the stairs and went into her room. She didn't want to see Ginny until she had time to calm down. The man is incredible, she told herself. Expecting me to explain . . .

Her harsh feelings ebbed. Perhaps she did owe him an explanation, she conceded. And if he had asked for one like a rational, reasonable human being, she might have been able to give him one. But under the circumstances, it was impossible. What had happened to him? Sarah asked herself forlornly. She yanked the sheet up and smoothed the bedspread. Yesterday he had been so warm, so gentle. But this morning all that had changed. The man she had come to like had evaporated. Had he seen her disappearance last night as a rejection, she asked herself. Was that what was making him act this way?

Sarah wasn't completely satisfied with that explanation of David's change in personality. However, she didn't know what else could have caused it. In a thoughtful mood she went down to find Ginny. Her own behavior was nothing to be proud of, but David's conduct had hurt Ginny. Again she told herself that she was better off not getting involved with a man like that. He had said himself that she had no place in his scheme of things. And, after the childish way he rushed out of the Gull's Nest that morning, she saw more clearly just how much he could hurt her.

Ginny was standing in front of the house next door, talking to a little girl. Sarah didn't call her. Making a new friend was more important than going to Rehoboth. They could go any time. Instead she made herself a cup of tea and tried to convince herself that she was not the least bit interested in David.

"Sarah," Ginny called. She and the little girl from next door came in through the kitchen door. "This is Kathy. She's spending the summer at the beach, too."

"Hello, Kathy," Sarah said. "It will be nice for Ginny to have a friend. Do you come to the beach every summer?"

"Yeah," she said. "My father's a writer, and he likes to work here."

"Oh, what does he write?"

Kathy shrugged. "Stuff for magazines mostly."

"What about your mother?" Sarah asked.

"I don't have one. She died when I was a baby."

"We want to go swimming," Ginny said before Sarah could ask any more questions. "Is it all right?"

"Sure," Sarah said. "I'll put my suit on, too, and join you, if I may."

"Meet you out on the beach," Kathy cried as she raced out the door.

"You don't mind if we don't go to Rehoboth, do you?" Ginny asked, sounding very grownup all of a sudden.

Sarah laughed. "I was only going for you. I don't mind at all." She rumpled Ginny's hair as they went upstairs to change their clothes. "We'll go another day. After all, we have the whole summer." She was glad to see that Ginny had gotten over her uncle's departure. Having a friend at the beach was going to be a big help.

"Don't go too far out," Sarah cautioned later as Ginny ran ahead of her toward Kathy and the water.

"We won't," they promised in a chorus.

Sarah opened her beach chair and began spreading sunscreen over her body. Although she was determined not to think of David, she couldn't help remembering how only yesterday he had smoothed the lotion over her body. The touch of his hands had made her weak. Even now, just the thought of his fingers on her body was enough to make her tremble with longing.

How many women has he brought to the beach, Sarah asked herself savagely, trying to distract her thoughts. How many women have enjoyed the same sensations? She was determined to forget the way he made her feel, determined to forget that she had any feeling for him at all.

"Do you mind if I sit with you?" a voice asked from above.

Sarah squinted up. A man in blue swimming trunks and a T-shirt was standing over her. He dropped down beside her without waiting for an answer. He had short, sandy hair and a friendly, open face. His eyes were blue, with laugh lines around the corners.

"I'm Ken Roberts," he said. "Kathy's father."

"I'm Sarah Bennet."

"It looks as though we're next-door neighbors," he said, looking at her approvingly. "Are you going to be here all summer?"

"All summer," Sarah said. "Unless Ginny gets tired of the beach—something I can't imagine happening."

"I'll hope that she doesn't," Ken said. "I think I'm going to like having you next door."

"Kathy says you're a writer," Sarah said. She wanted to change the subject. "Your name sounds familiar. What kind of things do you write?"

"I write a little of everything," he said vaguely. "Politics, economics, whatever strikes my fancy. You may have seen one of my articles in a magazine."

"Very probably."

"Tell me about yourself," Ken suggested. He gave her a friendly smile. "You can't be Ginny's mother."

Sarah shook her head. "No, I'm just a friend. I'm looking after her for the summer. Both her parents are dead."

"She's lucky to have you to look after her." Again he gave her an approving look. "Tell me, wasn't that David de Courcey I saw with the two of you yesterday?"

"Yes, it was. He's Ginny's uncle. Do you know him?"

"Not personally, but I know of him. From what I've heard, I wouldn't have thought he was the type to romp on the beach with a little girl. I certainly was wrong."

"Actually, he's quite good with Ginny," Sarah said carefully. She wasn't going to criticize David's relationship with Ginny to a stranger no matter how she felt about it personally.

"What about de Courcey and you?" he asked. "I'm

not prying," he said hastily as the expression on her face changed. "I was just wondering if there was anything between the two of you. I wouldn't want to step on any toes."

"There is nothing between us," Sarah said firmly. "David and I are just friends." And not very good friends at that, Sarah added to herself.

"Good," Ken said irrepressibly. "That's all the better for me."

Sarah couldn't help smiling. After David's complex personality, Ken's openness was a relief.

"What are you doing tonight?" he asked. "We could have a nice, romantic dinner on my deck. Just the four of us," he added as Ginny and Kathy came racing up.

Sarah laughed. "That sounds like fun." It did sound like fun. Sarah could see nothing of David in Ken Roberts. More importantly, she liked him but wasn't attracted to him in the least. He was the kind of man who could make the summer more interesting, without making it emotionally complicated. She didn't need any more emotional complications. Thanks to David, she had plenty of those.

Days, then weeks, began to pass. Sarah and Ginny settled down to the slow, lazy routine of beach life. Ginny and Kathy became almost inseparable, something Sarah welcomed for Ginny's sake and disliked for her own. With Ginny giggling and playing with Kathy most of the day, Sarah had too much time to think of David. As each day passed with no word from him, she tried to convince herself that he meant nothing to her. It wasn't easy. In fact, it was close to impossible. Carefully, analytically, she tried to discover what there was about him that had made such an impact on her.

She was sexually attracted to him, that much was obvious. But her feelings for David, whatever they were, were more than that. She had honestly liked the man he had become during those brief days when they had first arrived at the Gull's Nest. In Washington, too, though she hadn't exactly liked him, she had found him compelling.

Once the days began turning to weeks, a little of Sarah's anger returned. It was one thing for David to ignore her, but it was another for him to ignore Ginny. Though Ginny hadn't said anything about David's absence, Sarah knew she was unhappy with the fact that he was gone.

When Sarah got right down to it, she couldn't understand what was keeping David away. He had seemed to enjoy being with Ginny and playing with her at the beginning of the summer. Surely his enthusiasm, his friendliness hadn't been assumed. Why then, hadn't he come back? Sarah could answer that without thinking. It was his job. She knew that his work meant more to him than anything—or anyone. He had proved that before, and he was doing it again.

She thanked her lucky stars she had gone to her room that night rather than going back upstairs. Imagine if she had let passion override her common sense, she told herself, and his conquest made, he had left the next morning anyway. Just the thought of it turned her blood cold. She'd be feeling cheated and used, even more like a fool than she did now. One night of passion, or even a summer of passion wasn't worth the tears she would ultimately shed if she allowed herself to become involved with David. The price of an affair with him was too high, and she had no intention of paying it.

Though she used these arguments over and over, though she tried to convince herself that she only wanted him to return because of Ginny, it was a losing battle. At three in the morning, when she remembered the feel of his arms around her, she realized how much she wanted to see him.

In something akin to desperation, she agreed now and then to go out with Ken. One of the women in a nearby cottage had offered to look after both girls occasionally, taking away Sarah's last excuse. Although she enjoyed her evenings out, at a movie or dinner, she couldn't bring herself to feel anything more than friendliness for Ken. He was fun, she enjoyed his company, but he wasn't David.

No one could compare to David, she told herself. For better or worse, and it was usually for worse, he was unique. It has been more than four weeks since he walked out, Sarah thought late one afternoon as she was getting out the lettuce for salad. Over four weeks and she still couldn't forget him. If anything, she thought more about him as each day went by.

Her spirits were a little low. Ken had let her know, subtly but unmistakably, that he was only waiting for the go-ahead signal from her before he began to court her in earnest. Sarah knew that the wisest thing she could do would be to fall in love with someone like Ken, but after knowing David . . .

This is what you get for wishing for romance and excitement, Sarah told herself as she washed the lettuce. A handsome man walks into your life, whisks you off to his beautiful beach house, tries his best to make passionate love to you and what have you got? Misery . . . unhappiness. She dried her hands, went over to the refrigerator and rummaged around, looking for salad ingredients. The kitchen door opened behind her.

"Ginny, honey, would you set the table?" she asked. "I'll have the salad ready in a few minutes."

She had a bowl of tomatoes, green peppers, cucumbers, mushrooms, zucchini and a wedge of cheese balanced precariously in her arms as she turned. Standing in the doorway, watching her, stood not Ginny, but David himself.

For a moment Sarah couldn't believe he was real. She had been thinking of him so much, she had the idea she had conjured him up. The zucchini and green peppers began to tilt dangerously as she stared at him.

He looked as though he had come straight from the office. He was wearing a suit, but the shirt sleeves were rolled up and the suit jacket was tossed carelessly over his shoulder. His face was drawn, and his eyes had shadowy circles under them. He was obviously worn out.

Then her heart bounded, and she noticed nothing but her happiness at seeing him. Quickly she righted the slipping vegetables and tried to subdue the leaping of her heart. "Well," she said as she put the vegetables on the counter. "You're back."

She wondered if he could hear the happiness in her voice. It seemed obvious enough to her. She also wondered how he would treat her. They hadn't exactly parted on cordial terms.

"I called a couple of times this afternoon to tell you I was coming," he said, "but no one answered." His tone was not formal; neither was it particularly friendly.

"We were out on the beach most of the afternoon," Sarah said. "I'm sorry we didn't hear the phone."

"That's all right. I just wanted to tell you not to prepare any dinner. We can go out if you'd rather."

On the surface there was nothing wrong with the conversation. Both Sarah and David were being polite; both were speaking in neutral tones. But, as Sarah listened to him, she began to ache inside. Apparently there was no way they were going to be able to go back to the relationship they had before he had returned to Washington. That was over. She hadn't realized just how much she was hoping to re-establish the rapport between them until she saw how impossible that would be. Still, she couldn't help trying.

"You look tired," she said impulsively. "I'm sure you don't want to have to find a restaurant after such a long day. Wouldn't you rather eat here? I have some fish in the refrigerator. I'll broil that for you."

He gave her a tight smile, the kind he would give an

out-of-favor employee. Sarah tried not to let it affect her.

"I am tired," he confessed. "The last few weeks have been hectic. With almost everyone out of Washington for the summer, you wouldn't think there would be much going on, but there is."

"Why don't you go take a shower," Sarah suggested. She forced her mind to dwell on practical things. "I'll have some lemonade waiting for you when you're finished. You can sit out on the deck and drink it. Ginny should be back soon. She's going to be thrilled to see you."

Sarah smiled at him, hoping to see some warmth in his face. After all, if she could bury the hatchet, surely he could, too.

"Where is she?" he asked.

"Next door. She's made a friend."

"Good." He looked as though he was going to say something more. Sarah looked at him expectantly.

"I think I will have a shower," he said. Without another word, he left the room.

Sarah felt a flicker of disappointment. She had hoped he was going to say something more personal. Immediately she chided herself. She should consider herself lucky, she told herself, if he kept up this kind of polite friendliness. She had already seen just how vulnerable she was to his studied charm. No, this was safer. She didn't like it, but it was safer.

Again the kitchen door opened. This time it was Ginny. "Uncle David's car is in the driveway," she said breathlessly. It was obvious she had run home the moment she had seen it. "Is he here?"

"He is indeed." Sarah couldn't help smiling at her. She was as thrilled as Sarah had predicted she would be. "He's in the shower. Why don't you set the table? Then you can go out on deck and have some lemonade with him before dinner."

"When did he get here? How long can he stay?" Ginny bombarded her with questions.

"He just got here, and I don't know how long he's going to stay. You'll have to ask him."

"Ask him what?" David said.

Ginny shrieked and, much to Sarah's surprise, threw herself into David's arms. She has come a long way, Sarah thought, from the little girl who had been afraid to let her uncle see how much she needed him. Sarah was glad to see Ginny's spontaneous burst of emotion. It showed she didn't hold a month's disappearance against him. It seemed she was willing to try to improve their relationship. Over Ginny's head, David's eyes met hers briefly. He was as surprised as she was by Ginny's display of affection, but Sarah could see that he was touched by it.

"How long are you staying?" Ginny asked right away.

"At least two weeks," he told her.

Sarah's heart leaped. In two weeks they might be able to . . . she shut down that line of thought before it went any further.

"Two whole weeks?" Ginny sounded elated.

"Barring any unforeseen emergencies at the office," he amended.

Sarah frowned at that. Surely he could get away for two weeks. She had been away from Washington for nearly five weeks now, and her business hadn't gone under. She sighed, and some of the happiness she was feeling abated. Nothing had changed. As usual, his business came first.

"Here," she said, handing a glass to Ginny. "You and your uncle go sit on the deck. You can tell him what you've been doing while he's been gone. I made you a wine spritzer," she said to David. "I thought you'd rather have that than lemonade."

"Thanks," he said. "I would."

For a moment Sarah thought she saw a flicker of

warmth in his face, but it was gone so quickly she couldn't be sure. As she broiled the flounder, Sarah could hear their voices floating in through the window. Ginny was talking and laughing excitedly, and David sounded more relaxed. If she hadn't been so busy thinking of other things, she would have congratulated herself on how well they were getting along.

So glad had she been to see David that her heart had actually stopped when she turned from the refrigerator and found him standing there. She warned herself to be careful. She couldn't afford a repeat of what had happened before he left. If she found herself in his arms a second time, she might not have the strength to tear herself away.

"Who is this little girl Ginny keeps talking about?" David asked. He was helping her with the dishes while Ginny got ready for bed. Though Sarah had protested, David had insisted and so here they were, making small talk with one another.

"Kathy Roberts," Sarah told him. "She lives next door."

"I know where she lives. That's not what I meant. You have, I assume, met her parents."

"Of course I have," Sarah said indignantly. Surely after all this time he realized that she took her responsibilities seriously. "That is, I've met her father. She doesn't have a mother. Her father recognized you the last time you were here," Sarah added.

"Recognized me?" David frowned. "Who is he?"

"Ken Roberts. He's some kind of a writer."

"Ken Roberts is staying next door?" David sounded incredulous. "And his daughter and Ginny are good friends?"

"Yes, they are." Sarah looked at him in surprise. "Is there anything wrong with that?"

"I hope not," he said. The frown was still in his voice.

"I'm ready for bed," Ginny said behind them. "Can't

I stay up later tonight since it's Uncle David's first night?"

"You may not," Sarah said firmly. "Your uncle is tired and wants to go to bed himself. Besides, I'm sure tomorrow is going to be a full day."

"Will you tuck me in, Uncle David?" Ginny asked shyly.

"I'd be delighted," he said formally. Ginny giggled and took him by the hand.

Sarah watched them go with an inward smile. She didn't suppose any of David's business associates could imagine him tucking in a ten-year-old girl.

She hurried off to bed herself. She did not want to be alone with David. In her bed, with the moonlight streaming in through the window, Sarah thought of the way her heart had acted at the sight of him. She also thought of how the cool neutrality of his voice had sent her spirits plummeting.

As she lay there trying not to imagine him sleeping just down the hall, she came face-to-face with the question she had been avoiding all these long weeks. Had she fallen in love with David de Courcey?

Chapter Seven

"Uncle David, this is Kathy," Ginny said, dragging the other girl through the back door. "She's my best friend."

Sarah was glad to see them. David had been sitting at the table in the kitchen eating breakfast in complete silence while she put the dishes from Ginny's breakfast and her own in the dishwasher. She could think of nothing to say to him, and apparently he had nothing to say to her.

"Hello, Kathy," David said.

"I told Kathy you'd go out on the beach with us this morning," Ginny said. It was obvious she wanted to show her uncle off. "You will, won't you?"

"Of course I will. And this afternoon I thought we'd drive up to Rehoboth. I haven't forgotten that I owe you an afternoon on the boardwalk."

From her position by the sink, Sarah looked at him in surprise. She hadn't expected him to remember that.

"Can Kathy come, too?" Ginny asked.

"If her father says she can." There was a note to David's voice that Sarah didn't understand. "Though I'm sure he won't have any objections."

"And Sarah, too?"

"Why not?" David said lightly. "Unless Sarah has something she'd rather do."

This time Sarah understood his tone of voice. There was no misunderstanding it. He didn't want her along and he was subtly telling her so. Her back stiffened. She didn't want to go any more than he wanted her to. She was about to make some excuse when a voice floated in through the open doorway.

"Sarah," it said. "Have you seen my daughter?"

"That's my daddy," Kathy said unnecessarily.

Ken came to the door, opened it and stepped inside. "I turned my back for a moment and she was gone." He saw David sitting at the table. "Sorry. I didn't realize . . ."

"I'm sure you didn't." There was sarcasm in David's voice as he interrupted the other man. "You must be Ken Roberts." He got to his feet. "I'm David de Courcey," he said with a coldness which didn't deceive anyone. He was angry about something though Sarah couldn't possibly imagine what it was. The two men shook hands warily.

"I'll meet you on the beach," David told Ginny. "Give me a few minutes to change." Without another word, he turned on his heel and walked out of the room.

Sarah was dumbfounded by his rudeness. What had gotten into him?

"Go on outside, kids," Ken said to the two girls. "I want to talk to Sarah." He let out a long whistle as the door closed behind them. "What's the matter with him?" he asked, referring to David.

Sarah shrugged her shoulders. She couldn't think of any way to explain David's behavior to Ken, or to herself. What *had* gotten into him?

"Maybe he doesn't like me hanging around you," Ken speculated. He gave her a sharp glance.

"Don't be silly. I told you, he and I are just friends," Sarah said firmly.

If only she could attribute David's bad manners to jealousy. But no, that was out of the question. David didn't care enough about her to be jealous while she . . .

"Well," Ken was saying, "if he's always like that, I feel sorry for Ginny—and for you. I must say, though, what I saw just a few minutes ago was more in keeping with his reputation than this role he's playing of the devoted uncle."

"It's not a role," Sarah said quickly. She felt she had to defend David. She wanted to defend him. "He is devoted to Ginny." In his own way, she added to herself.

Ken looked skeptical. "From what I've heard, he's devoted to his work and nothing more. Nothing and no one, including a cute little girl like Ginny, would ever be allowed to interfere with that."

Again Sarah rushed to David's defense. She didn't want Ken to know how close he was to the truth. "That's obviously not true," she said coolly. "You know how exaggerated rumors can be," she added, making her voice a little warmer.

Ken looked unconvinced. "I know one thing. I'm going to make myself scarce while he's around. It's obvious I'm persona non grata as far as he's concerned. How long will he be here?"

"He said a couple of weeks," Sarah said.

Ken groaned and gave her a look of mock despair. "That long? Okay, Sarah, I'll see you then."

Sarah laughed in spite of herself. "We'll see each other on the beach," she called after him. Alone again, she finished the dishes and wondered what she should do during the day. Only one thing was certain. She wanted to avoid David at all costs. Discovering she had fallen in love with him was painful enough. There was no reason to rub salt in an open wound.

No, he and Ginny could spend most of the next two weeks together. That was what she wanted, anyway, she told herself. She wanted Ginny and David to grow closer. She hoped David would learn to love Ginny so that he would be willing to provide her with the kind of home she should have. Compared to Ginny's needs, her own feelings didn't matter much, Sarah thought a little sadly.

"Has he gone?" David asked. He had come back into the kitchen dressed in swimming trunks and a T-shirt. Sarah's heart skipped a beat as she looked up at him. With his long, muscular legs and broad shoulders, he was made for casual clothes.

"He's gone," she answered evenly. "You certainly weren't very polite. In fact, you were downright rude." The words seemed to slip out on their own. Sarah had already decided not to mention the way he had treated Ken. Things were bad enough between the two of them of them without adding an argument over Ken to the list.

"He doesn't deserve anything else," David said crisply. "He's lucky I didn't throw him out of the house."

"Why?" Sarah was bewildered. "What's he done?"

"You mean he hasn't mentioned it to you?"

"No. I don't know what you're talking about."

David gave her a skeptical look. "I find that hard to believe. Why don't you ask him? You two seem to be such good friends." He put a faint emphasis on the words good friends.

"We are friends," Sarah said with dignity. "For that reason I'd rather you tell me what it is you think he's done. He didn't have the faintest idea why you were so rude," she added.

"Oh, he didn't?" David's tone was withering. "Don't

be naive, Sarah. Ken Roberts knows exactly what he's doing and exactly what the consequences might be."

Sarah made an impatient gesture. "What is it that he's done?"

"You do know that he's a journalist, don't you?"

"I know he's some kind of writer, but I don't know much about politics so I'm not familiar with his work."

"Well, then, I'll tell you about his work. He's the worst kind of journalist there is. He digs up all the dirt he can about his subject then uses every rumor, every innuendo he can find when he writes about them. As far as he's concerned, the juicier the story, the better he likes it—no matter whether or not he's printing the truth."

Sarah stared at him. She was aghast at his words. "I can't believe that," she said finally. "He's such a nice person."

"Let me tell you something else," David said coldly. He was obviously angry. "All spring he camped out at my office, hoping I'd give him an interview."

"And did you?"

"Of course not."

Sarah shook her head. None of what he was telling her squared with the Ken Roberts she knew.

"For all I know," David went on, "he learned about the Gull's Nest, then rented the house next door hoping to meet me socially. If that was his plan, it worked out better than he hoped. His little girl has made friends with Ginny while he has become friendly, quite friendly, from the looks of it, with you. Who knows what kind of information you two have unwittingly been feeding him?"

Sarah looked at him in disbelief. "You can't believe he'd use his little girl to get information about you?"

"I can believe anything about Ken Roberts, and if you'd read any of the articles he writes, you'd believe it too."

"I'm sorry," Sarah said quietly, "but I think you're wrong. He hasn't once asked me about you. In fact, we haven't discussed you at all."

She was beginning to feel a little sorry for David. He lived in a different world than she did, and in his world there obviously wasn't much room for trust.

"Just you wait," David said bitingly. "He will. Now, I'm going out to the beach."

Sarah took a large sketchpad upstairs where she could work and watch David from the balcony at the same time. She was angry with him, she felt sorry for him—yet in spite of her confusion, she wanted to be out on the beach with him. She wanted to recapture the magic they had shared during those first few days of summer. Since she knew that was impossible, she had to content herself with watching him from the balcony. At least she could see him, and that was better than nothing.

The ringing of the telephone brought her inside. It was David's secretary. Sarah told her David was out.

"I must get in touch with him," the woman said worriedly. Please ask him to call me as soon as he gets in. It's urgent."

Sarah took the message with a sinking heart. She stood by the phone for a moment debating whether or not to go out to the beach and tell him of the call. In the end, she decided not to. Whatever it was could wait. Ginny was more important.

Two hours later, she was having second thoughts. He would be furious when he learned she had kept an important message from him.

"Your secretary called," Sarah told him as soon as they came in.

"When?"

"About ten."

"That was two hours ago," he exclaimed. "Why didn't you come out and tell me?"

"You looked like you were having so much fun I didn't want to interrupt," Sarah said calmly.

The look on his face was making her feel guilty. Perhaps she should have told him at once. Then she remembered the happiness on Ginny's face as they had come into the house. No, she was glad she had waited.

David went into his study and called his office. When he came back he seemed preoccupied.

"I've got to go back to Washington for a few days," he announced. "A cabinet minister from one of the African nations is coming to town, and he wants to see me."

"But you just got here," Ginny said. She looked as though she were about to cry. "You can't leave."

"I'm sorry, Ginny, but I have to. I won't be gone long," he promised. "I'll be back before you know it."

"I don't want you to leave." The tears began to spill over.

"There's nothing I can do about it," he said, giving her an irritated look.

Ginny ran out of the room sobbing. Sarah could hear her running up the stairs to her room. David looked after her helplessly.

"Explain it to her," he said to Sarah. "I don't have time."

"I can't explain it to her," Sarah told him, "because I don't understand it myself. Why do you have to leave?"

"I told you," he said impatiently, "an important dignitary from another country . . ."

"Don't you have an associate who can see him?" Sarah interrupted. Her questions, accusations really, seemed to tumble out one after the other. "Why do you have to rush back to Washington? Can't you see how upset Ginny is? Is that man more important to you than she is?"

"You know how much my work means to me," he said. His tone was icy.

"Yes, I do. But it seems to me this is one time you ought to find someone else to take your place. If you'd learn to delegate a little responsibility, you wouldn't have to be on the spot all the time. That would be better for Ginny, and you," Sarah told him, throwing tact out the window.

"You're here to look after Ginny, not to tell me what's best for me or how to run my company."

Clearly she had made him angry. Sarah gulped. She knew she had no business talking to him this way but she couldn't stand by and watch Ginny be hurt. Especially not now that she knew how loving and affectionate David could be.

"I'm not trying to tell you how to run your business," Sarah said, trying to hold on to the edges of her temper. "But I want you to understand just how hard all this coming and going is on Ginny. You saw how happy and excited she was yesterday when you arrived and how devastated she was when you said you had to leave. Doesn't that make you feel the least bit guilty for running out on her?"

"I'm not running out on her." If anything, David's voice had grown colder. His eyes flashed with black anger. "I will be back as soon as I can. It's up to you to make her understand that."

"I'll try," Sarah said. She was now as furious as he was. "But I don't think I'll have much luck. The last time you were called away, you didn't return for a month. How am I going to convince her this time is different?"

"I don't have time to argue with you." David turned sharply and started out of the room.

As Sarah watched him start up the stairs, she felt compunction sweep over her. Why hadn't she handled him with more tact? Why hadn't she chosen her words more carefully? If he left like this, angry as he was, he might not want to come back.

"David," she said, trying to steady the anger in her voice. "Wait, please."

He stopped and looked at her over the bannister.

"I'm not trying to make you angry," she told him as calmly as she could. "I'm just trying to make you understand that you're going to have to face your responsibility to Ginny, or you're going to lose her completely. I don't want to see that happen. I know you care for her in your own way."

His eyes were unreadable. Sarah couldn't tell if she had made an impression or not, though his next words made her think she had wasted her breath.

"I'll be back as soon as I can." His voice was implacable, and Sarah knew she could say nothing which would change his mind.

She waited until she heard the door to his room close, then she flew up the stairs to comfort Ginny. Ginny was curled up in a ball on the bed, crying into her pillow.

Sarah leaned over and put her arms around the little girl. "He'll be back as soon as he can," she whispered, unconsciously echoing David's words. As she spoke, she hoped she wasn't making things worse. Would he come back? "I had a little talk with him after you left the room and he promised."

"He promises lots of things, but he never means them," the little girl sobbed. "He just doesn't like me and I don't like him either. I hope he never comes back."

Sarah's arms tightened around Ginny. She felt tears form in her own eyes, and she wondered what she could say to comfort Ginny. This time David had really hurt her.

"That's not true and you know it. Your uncle loves you very much. He just doesn't understand how much you need him. You're going to have to give him a little time, Ginny. He's got to learn how to be an uncle, and you've got to teach him."

"Do you really think he'll be back soon? Last time he was gone for almost five weeks. I know. I counted."

The simplicity of her words touched Sarah. "Yes," she said, "I really do think he'll be back soon. Now you go splash some water on your face, and we'll go down and say good-bye to him." He will be back soon, she vowed to herself, even if I have to go to Washington myself and bring him back.

Obediently, Ginny went into the bathroom and washed her face in cold water. Her eyes were red and swollen when she came back in the room, but she had stopped crying. Hand-in-hand they went downstairs.

David was just leaving. He looked surprised when he saw the two of them coming down the steps. He immediately went over to Ginny and gave her a kiss on the cheek.

"I really am sorry I have to leave," he told her. "I'll be back as quickly as I can."

"Do you promise?" Ginny asked.

"I promise," he said kindly. He knelt down beside her. "You know, while I was upstairs getting dressed I had a thought. Instead of going to Rehoboth when I get back, we'll go to Ocean City. The boardwalk there has a roller coaster, a ferris wheel and lots of other rides. Would you like to go there instead?"

"That sounds super." Ginny was beginning to sound a little more like herself. She gave her uncle a hug. "Come back soon," she told him.

"I will." He got to his feet and his eyes met Sarah's over Ginny's head. "Good-bye, Sarah."

"Good-bye," she echoed as he closed the door behind him.

She stared at his retreating back through the screen door, wishing they had parted on more cordial terms. Of course, she was glad he and Ginny had reached some kind of understanding. She only wished she could do the same thing.

"I'd better go tell Kathy we can't go to Rehoboth this afternoon," Ginny said a little wistfully.

"There's no need to do that," Sarah said. "I'll take you."

Suddenly she wanted to get away from the Gull's Nest. She wanted to go some place where she wouldn't be reminded of David. Here his personality filled every room. On the crowded boardwalk at Rehoboth, she could forget David, forget the feelings he stirred up in her. At least she hoped she could. David had made such an impact that it wouldn't be easy. Though he had been there for less than twenty-four hours, he had managed to turn first her world topsy-turvy, then Ginny's.

The two of them walked over to the cottage next door. When Ken appeared, Sarah looked at him searchingly. Could he really be here in search of a story? One look at his face told her otherwise. David was so complicated a person that he expected other people to be as complicated. She remembered the almost sinister motives he had attributed to her when she had taken Ginny in and decided he was probably being equally unfair to Ken. Anyway, she wasn't going to let David's words poison her friendship with Ken.

"I'm going to be taking the two girls to Rehoboth," she told him. "We'll go as soon as Kathy's ready."

Ken looked down at Ginny's red and puffy face. It was obvious that she had been crying.

"Oh?" was all he said, but Sarah knew he was wondering what had happened. While she was trying to decide how much explaining she ought to do, Ginny spoke up.

"Uncle David had to go back to Washington," she told Ken. "He's very important, you know."

Sarah could see that Ken was suppressing a smile. She could also see that he connected Ginny's tear-swollen eyes with her uncle's departure.

"I'm sure he is," he said gravely. "I tell you what let's do. I'll come with you, and we'll have an early dinner in Rehoboth, then go to a movie. Would you like that?"

"Can Kathy and I choose the movie?" Ginny asked.

Ken groaned. "I'll probably be sorry I said yes, but yes, you can." He opened the screen door. "Go on in and tell Kathy to hurry up."

"She looked pretty upset," he said, stepping outside. "I hope you don't mind me inviting myself along. I just thought we could cheer her up."

"Of course I don't mind."

He looked at her curiously, obviously expecting her to say more to explain Ginny's unhappiness.

"She was a little upset when her uncle said he had to go back to Washington, but I think she's over it now." Sarah was feeling distinctly uncomfortable. In spite of herself, she couldn't help remembering David's words. Was Ken probing for something he could use in an article?

"Ginny's loss is my gain," he said. "I, for one, am not sorry to see him go. Tonight we'll devote to the kids, and tomorrow night I'll take you out to a really nice restaurant. You look as though you could use an evening out yourself. I'm sure having David de Courcey in the house is no picnic."

"He's quite tame, actually," Sarah said lightly. She was annoyed with Ken for criticizing David, however obliquely. She was also annoyed with David for planting suspicions of Ken in her mind. David certainly knows how to complicate things, she told herself crossly. When that man is involved, nothing is simple. She wondered why it was that she was so in love with him. He certainly hadn't been very loveable lately.

"Well, what do you say?" Ken was asking. "Would you like to go out to dinner tomorrow night? I'll get Mrs. Johnson to look after the kids."

"Yes, I would," Sarah said half-heartedly. What she

really wanted was a quiet, intimate dinner with David, unwise though she knew it to be. She heard the lack of enthusiasm in her voice and gave Ken a warm smile to make up for it. No matter what David said, she thought defiantly, she genuinely liked him.

"Good," Ken told her. "It's a deal."

"You look beautiful," Ginny said admiringly. She was lying on her stomach on Sarah's bed watching her get dressed.

Sarah had just slipped into a filmy white dress, trimmed with crocheted edgings. The dress had an elasticized neckline which Sarah wore pulled down off her shoulders. Though it wasn't a particularly high-fashion look, it was one Sarah enjoyed for the summer. The white of the dress showed off her tan, and the lace and ruffles added a note of romance. She felt entirely feminine in the dress and very pretty.

"Thank you very much," Sarah told her. "What do you think of this?" She held up a small sand dollar which had been dipped in gold. She had bought one for herself and one for Ginny yesterday while they were walking on the boardwalk in Rehoboth.

"That's perfect."

Sarah fastened it around her neck. "Why don't you go next door and tell Ken I'll be over in a few minutes. I'm running a little bit late."

Ginny hopped off the bed. "Okay."

Sarah smiled as she heard Ginny clatter down the stairs. Then her smile faded. Not a word from David. Sarah had hoped he would have called by now to give them an idea of when he would be back. If he didn't call by tomorrow evening, she told herself, she would call him.

Sarah brushed her hair vigorously, then decided to wear it up. With her hair piled on top of her head, she liked the way the dress showed off the lines of her neck and shoulders. Deftly she brushed her hair into a smooth chignon, making sure a few tendrils of hair escaped to curl around her face. She was just giving herself a last glance of approval in the mirror when she heard the front screen door slam shut.

"Ken?" she called down the stairs. He must have gotten tired of waiting for her. "I'll be right down."

She went back to her room, picked up her pocket-book and a silky shawl and turned toward the door. She gasped. Standing in the door frame, nearly filling it, was David, not Ken. Her heart began to flutter from the simple joy of seeing him.

"I thought you were Ken," she said confusedly.

"Obviously. Does he come up to your bedroom often?"

Sarah blushed and the joy she was experiencing diminished considerably. "You know he doesn't," she said coldly. "We have a dinner date, and I'm running a little late. Naturally when I heard the door slam, I thought it was Ken." She still hadn't recovered from her surprise at seeing him. Surely he couldn't have finished his business in Washington so quickly. "We didn't expect you back so soon," she told him. Should she cancel her dinner date? she was asking herself.

"That, too, is obvious. But I did say I'd be back as soon as I could. Where is Ginny, by the way?"

"She's next door. An older woman from one of the cottages a few houses down is staying with the two girls this evening," she hastened to explain. She had the feeling David was not going to approve of this arrangement. She was right.

"Who is this woman?" he asked suspiciously.

"She's a very nice, very respectable woman who enjoys looking after the girls. She says they remind her of her grandchildren. You needn't worry. I wouldn't leave Ginny if I thought there was anything the least bit questionable about Mrs. Johnson." Sarah didn't like the way David was putting her on the defensive.

"It sounds as though you've left Ginny with this Mrs. Johnson before."

Sarah nodded warily. "I have, but only two or three times at the most."

"While you were going out with Ken?"

"Yes."

He leaned against the door jamb lazily. Sarah couldn't tell exactly what he was thinking, but she could tell she had made him angry. She always seemed to make him angry, she thought miserably. She was sorry now she had accepted Ken's dinner invitation. She wouldn't have if she'd known David would be back.

"After what I told you, I'm surprised that you're having dinner with a man like Ken Roberts," David said. "I thought you had more sense than that."

"I think you're wrong about him," she said evenly. All thoughts of canceling the date left her mind. If she stayed here, she and David would just end up arguing.

"You're being naive," he told her softly. "Can't you see he's just using you to get information about me?"

Anger flared in Sarah. Didn't he think she could attract a man on her own? "That's not so," she said heatedly. "In the first place, we don't even talk about you and in the second place, I don't have any information to give him. You're being . . ." she fumbled for a word.

"Paranoid?" he asked dangerously.

She gave him an even look. "Yes, paranoid. I've told you before that not everyone has an ulterior motive. You were wrong about me, and you're wrong about Ken."

"I didn't realize Ken was so important to you," David said suddenly.

"He's not."

"Then why are you defending him so vehemently?"

"Because you're being completely unfair. I've told you before that he and I are just friends." She was suddenly tired of this conversation. There was no reasoning with David and she was wasting her time trying. "I've got to go. I'm late as it is. Ginny's already eaten," she told him as he stepped aside so she could get through the door.

As she walked by him, she had an almost overwhelming urge to reach out and touch him, to use her lips for something other than arguing. Why did they always argue? she asked herself in anguish, when they could do so many other things? Because those other things were far more dangerous than arguing could ever be, she answered herself quickly. Still, she ached as she went by him, wishing it weren't so.

"I'll send Ginny home," she said over her shoulder. "If you're hungry, there's food in the refrigerator." Sarah left him standing in the door to her room.

"Your uncle is back," she said to Ginny as soon as she reached Kathy's house. "I told him you'd be right over."

"Are we still on?" Ken asked anxiously.

"Of course," Sarah said. She made an effort to smile at him. "Why not?" What she really wanted to do was go for a long walk by herself. She needed to sort through and settle down the conflicting emotions David always seemed to arouse.

He shrugged. "I thought you might have to fix him dinner or something."

"I'm not his housekeeper," Sarah said sharply. "He's perfectly capable of fixing his own dinner."

"Let's go then."

Despite her best intentions, the evening was not a success. She couldn't eat more than a few mouthfuls of the delicious food nor could she keep her mind on Ken's conversation. David filled her thoughts. She wished, how she wished, it was David sitting across from her in the candlelit restaurant. She sighed to herself, trying not to let Ken see how much she wanted to go home.

"You're back early," David said as she let herself into the house.

He was in the living room but whether he was waiting up for her, Sarah couldn't tell.

"Didn't you enjoy your date?"

"I had a very nice time, thank you," Sarah said coolly. She moved toward the stairs. "I think I'll go check on Ginny."

"That's not necessary. I looked in on her just a few minutes ago. She's sound asleep. Would you like some brandy?"

Though there wasn't much warmth in his voice, Sarah had the idea the offer of the brandy was an overture to friendship. She hesitated, wondering whether it might not be wiser just to say good night. If she stayed, they'd probably end up arguing, and she didn't think she could take much more of that. She opened her mouth to refuse.

"Yes, I would," her voice said instead. To her horror, she found herself walking into the living room and sitting down.

David handed her a large brandy snifter made of thin, fragile glass with a shimmering liquid at the bottom. Sarah swirled it around slowly, letting the air release the brandy's aroma.

What had possessed her to accept the drink? It seemed to anchor her to the living room. She had meant to go directly upstairs, and that is exactly what she should have done. What was she going to do now to keep herself from ending up in the one place she so desperately wanted to be—in his arms?

"Were you able to find something for dinner?" she asked, searching for a topic that wouldn't provoke an argument.

He ignored the question. Instead he sat down beside her on the sofa, closer than was necessary. Sarah shrank back a little. "Where did you have dinner?" he asked.

"At the Greenhouse," she said cautiously. She definitely did not want to talk about her evening. Not with David, not considering the kind of thing he might say about Ken.

"That's quite an elegant restaurant," David commented. "Ken was going all out. Did he finally get around to asking about me?"

Sarah stiffened. "No, he didn't," she said evenly. "We had other things to discuss."

"Such as?"

David sounded as if he really wanted to know, but Sarah wasn't about to tell him what they had talked about over dinner. "I really don't want to talk about Ken. We'll just end up arguing." She put down her glass of brandy. "Perhaps I should go on upstairs."

David stopped her. "Not yet," he said. "If you don't want to talk about Ken, let's talk about you." His arm stole across the back of the sofa and he lightly caressed her face with his fingers.

Sarah forced herself not to jump at the touch of his hand. "I don't want to talk about myself either," she said coolly. "There's obviously no point to this conversation so . . ."

He ignored her. "You're more beautiful than usual this evening." His fingers slid down her bare neck leaving little trails of fire behind them. "That dress suits you." His voice had grown soft, and something in his eyes had deepened.

Sarah's mouth had gone dry, and she watched him with a kind of helpless fascination. She sat quietly, letting his eyes sensuously probe her own, his hand stroke her bare shoulders.

"Your hair suits you, too," he went on. "I like it up like that." His large hand circled her slender neck, and he leaned forward to slowly and deliberately kiss her throat before his lips moved to her earlobe.

Sarah sat rigid, refusing to yield to the sensations his lips were causing. Though she wanted to press against him, she knew she had to resist the force of his desire, and hers. There was nothing to be gained by this kind of thing, she told herself in anguish—nothing but the pleasure of feeling his body pressed against hers. She clamped down on that feeling.

There was nothing to be gained, she repeated firmly while David's lips produced a heat in her body she was finding difficult to ignore. There was nothing to be gained but the heartache of being cast aside when the summer was over.

David continued to nibble at her neck. Hot chills were beginning to run up and down her body, and Sarah felt her willpower growing weaker. "Don't," she said suddenly.

David pulled away and looked deeply into her eyes.

Now was her chance, she told herself a little desperately. She tried to get up, but her body refused to obey the commands of her mind. Instead she gazed helplessly back into David's eyes.

"Why not?" he asked. "It's what we both want."

"It's not what I want," she told him with a firmness which surprised herself.

Get up, she thought. Leave the room before it's too late.

At her words, David's slow deliberation disappeared, and he pulled her into his arms almost roughly. Impatiently his lips sought hers. Sarah thought of resisting, but as their lips touched, she felt something like a sigh in her body. This was where she belonged. She melted against David, letting his tongue part her lips. There was an urgency to his lovemaking, an urgency which had been absent the other times he had kissed her.

Sarah felt herself respond to this new mood. Fire seemed to run through her veins as his tongue probed the sensitive skin of her mouth. She noticed her arms slipping around David's neck; she felt her hands stroking him in response. Then she noticed nothing more, for David's fingers began moving slowly down her body, leaving her weak with desire. Gently his hands moved down her back, across her hips and down her legs.

Through the light, cotton gauze of her dress, Sarah could feel the warmth of David's hands on her thighs. Her legs grew heavy as he touched them. Without stopping, his fingers trailed down to her knees. He slipped his hand underneath her dress and ran his fingers up and down her bare legs before he pulled her over his body so that she lay across his lap.

His lips left hers and began traveling down her neck, across her shoulders, then down toward her breast. Sarah's head fell back, and her body began to quiver under the force of his lips and hands. His lips continued downward, and Sarah moaned softly as she waited for them to touch her breast.

Instead, he recaptured her mouth with a possessiveness which scattered what was left of Sarah's common sense. In that moment she knew she would do nothing to stop him. She knew she wanted to belong to him completely, no matter what the consequences.

Joyfully, she returned the kiss. Joyfully, she matched his passion with passion of her own. As their tongues touched, though, something began to pull naggingly at the back of her mind. Sarah ignored it. She wanted to concentrate on the moment. She wanted nothing to interfere. For a few moments she succeeded. Then the thought came to her that David's lovemaking was a heavy, deliberate thing. While she was feeling rapture at the touch of his hands and a desire to share herself with him, she could sense none of that in his kisses. It was as if something else were driving him.

Quickly, and none too clearly, Sarah cast her mind back to the other times he had kissed her. No, this was not the same. Something was missing . . . something had been added, she wasn't sure which. If it hadn't been for that doubt tugging at the back of her mind, she wouldn't have cared.

David's hand moved slowly across her stomach, and Sarah felt her body twist toward him. For a moment, the doubt disappeared. Then he raised his head slightly. Sarah forced her eyes open. He gave her a dark look and her eyes closed again, almost in protection.

His lips moved to her shoulders. "Does Ken kiss you like this?" she heard him mutter. "Do you let him touch you like I do?"

Sarah froze, and the heat running through her veins changed to ice for a few seconds. Her mind was slower to react. Ken? she asked herself confusedly. What does he have to do with us? What does he have to do with anything? Her voice cried out in her mind, and for a moment she thought she had said the words out loud. Then she realized she couldn't have, for David was again kissing her with that devastating thoroughness.

That was what was wrong, Sarah thought as she struggled against the tide of David's passion. He was making love to her not out of any positive emotion, but out of a sense of . . . what? Not jealousy. Sarah could never make herself believe that, not after all the cold words they had exchanged. But what, then?

David's hands again began to wander along her body and Sarah had to struggle against being seduced by the sensations they produced. She tried to pull away from him, but she couldn't. Her body wasn't yet ready to obey the commands of her mind.

What was behind his lovemaking, she asked herself, as she desperately tried to keep her mind clear. Much as she wanted to, she couldn't give in to him. Not now that she knew he wasn't interested in sharing himself the way she was interested in sharing herself. His kisses were not prompted by love, they weren't even prompted by a simple desire. There was something else there, something more complicated, something hurtful.

She had it. Revenge. He was getting back at her, because she didn't believe the things he had said about Ken, because she had gone out with Ken in spite of his obvious wish that she avoid him. What better weapon could he use to punish her, she asked herself bitterly, than this one? He had seen before how she reacted to his kisses and the feel of his hands. Misery began washing over her, pushing out the desire which raged in her veins.

She had been prepared to give herself to him, prepared to love him as completely as a woman could love a man. But not now, she vowed. Not now.

David's hands ceased their wanderings. Again he raised his head and gave her that dark look. "Well," he asked hoarsely, "do you enjoy it when he kisses you? Do you enjoy it as much as this?"

The strength returned to Sarah's body. She pushed him away with all her might and swung her feet to the floor. Before he could react, she was standing in front of him, just out of his reach. She knew what she must look like. Her hair had come tumbling down, her dress was wrinkled and her lips were swollen by the force of his kisses.

"How can you even ask such questions?" she cried. She wanted to tell him of her love for him, to tell him that he was the only man in her world, the only man she had ever allowed to come so close. But she knew that would be the ultimate folly. Besides, he probably wouldn't believe her.

His eyes were cold as he watched her. "You've gone out with him several times," he said casually. "Naturally, I wondered what was going on while I was away."

David's tone was so offhanded that Sarah wanted to slap him as she had once before. She felt an unreasonable, and unreasoning, urge to hurt him as he was hurting her. Was he blind? Couldn't he see what he meant to her? Her eyes filled with tears, and she blinked them away furiously.

"Nothing has been going on," she told him. If he couldn't feel her love for him in the way she kissed him, the way her body bent to his, she could never make him understand that there was no other man in her life. Then she realized that he probably didn't care about those things. He had brought up Ken's name, he had used his kisses and his hands to hurt her, to pay her back for seeing a man he distrusted.

She didn't matter at all, not to David de Courcey. Nothing mattered to him but his job. Her tears threatened to spill over. Before he could see them, Sarah turned and left the room. As she hurried up the stairs to her room, she could imagine him sitting on the sofa watching her sardonically.

Miserably she undressed and slid into her bed. Tossing and turning, she waited for the sleep which was tortuously slow in coming.

Chapter Eight

The sun had just come up when Sarah slipped out of her bedroom and went downstairs. She had spent a restless night, haunted by the memory of David's lovemaking and troubled, too, by her own response to it. All through the long night she had agonized over her decision. Had she done the right thing?

Now, in the cool morning air, she was glad things had turned out as they had. Maybe not glad exactly, she corrected herself silently, but at least she recognized the wisdom in not allowing last night's fling to reach its natural culmination. She should never have fallen in love with David, she told herself, as though there had been a choice. What future was there in loving a man who put his career before all else as she had once done? What future was there in loving a man who was married to his work?

Falling in love with him was bad enough. Even worse, though, would have been giving herself to him. Under different circumstances it might be all right, but considering how desperately she loved him, she knew she could never indulge in a casual affair, one which would end with the arrival of fall.

For a few moments Sarah almost wished she were a different kind of person. One who could become involved in love affairs with no damage to her heart, one who treated physical pleasure as casually as David did. But, she thought with a sigh, she wasn't like that and she never would be. Wishing wouldn't make it so. She was Sarah Bennet, a woman to whom sex and love went hand-in-hand, and nothing would ever change that.

Quietly she stole out the back door, making sure to close it gently behind her. She didn't want to wake Ginny; she wanted to be alone. With any luck, the soothing motion of the waves and the solitude of the beach would calm her and help her see things with some kind of perspective.

She had just left behind the section of beach which was populated by houses when she heard a voice behind her. It was David's. As soon as she heard it, butterflies began flying about in her stomach. She pretended she didn't hear him and quickened her pace without making it seem obvious. She didn't want to see him. What could they possibly have to say to one another after last night?

David was not to be put off. He called to her again, more loudly this time. There was no way Sarah could not have heard him. She toyed with the idea of simply ignoring him, but she realized at once that that would never work. David was not the kind of man who let himself be ignored. Reluctantly she turned and waited for him to catch up to her. She watched him coming closer and closer, trying to view him objectively, trying to ignore the fact that her heart beat faster with each step he took.

"You're up early," he said as he reached her. "Do you mind if I walk with you?"

Sarah did mind but she didn't say so. She wanted to be alone and even if she weren't alone, the last person she wanted to be with was David. He was the very reason she had left the house so early in the morning. "I suppose not," she said with an inward sigh.

Together they walked farther away from the houses. Sarah went down the beach to the water and walked where the surf could splash on her feet. Paying no attention to David, she leaned over and slowly rolled up her khaki slacks so that they wouldn't get wet. She was half-hoping he'd get bored and go away. Instead he waited for her patiently and said not a word.

It wasn't until they had been walking for nearly a half hour that he spoke. "Let's go sit over there," he said, gesturing toward some highly banked sand dunes.

"No, thanks I came out here to walk," she told him briefly, "and that's what I intend to do. If you're tired, stop. I'll go on." She made a move to leave him behind.

"I want to talk to you," he said firmly, catching her arm and leading her away from the water.

A little angrily, Sarah shook her arm free. She didn't want him to touch her—not after last night. The memory of how close his touch had brought her to yielding to him was all too clear. However, she followed him reluctantly. What can happen on the beach? she asked herself. Before long there would be people about.

They sat down amidst the dunes where they could look out over the ocean. The beach was deserted. Sarah glanced at him. He was staring at the water with a pensive look on his face.

"What do you want to talk about?" she asked. She was hoping to get this discussion over as quickly as possible. Even though she had made sure there was a good distance between them, sitting next to him made her skin tingle. Could she handle him—and herself—if he tried to kiss her? She could, she told herself staunchly, and she would.

"I want to talk about last night."

Sarah was not surprised. He was probably going to demand an explanation for her behavior. It never seemed to occur to him that his own actions needed to be explained.

"I owe you an apology," he told her quietly. So quietly she almost didn't hear him.

Sarah was more than surprised, she was dumbfounded. This was the last thing she had expected to hear.

"I know you were angry with me for the things I said, and I don't blame you," he went on stiffly. He sounded as though he hadn't had much practice at apologizing.

And he probably hasn't, she thought to herself. She couldn't imagine him doing it often.

"What goes on between you and Ken is none of my business."

His voice had lost some of its stiffness and it had also grown louder, much louder. Sarah's heart sank. Were they going to argue again?

"I've told you before," she said wearily, "that nothing is going on between us. We're just friends."

He didn't answer. Sarah couldn't tell whether or not he believed her, but she didn't suppose it mattered one way or the other. She meant nothing to David. He had let her know that repeatedly. Each time she had begun to hope that something was developing between them, some kind of friendship or rapport, he would dash it. David didn't let people get close to him; he didn't even seem to want to.

"Is that all you wanted to talk about?" she asked as she started to get to her feet. There was no sense sitting here torturing herself by his closeness, she thought to herself. Though he had hurt her, hurt her deeply, she still wanted to be in his arms, to feel his lips pressed against hers.

"No, that's not all." He pulled her back down beside him. He didn't seem to notice how Sarah shrank from his touch. "I want to talk about Ginny."

"Yes?" Sarah asked cautiously. She had no idea what was coming now.

"I've been thinking about what to do with her once the summer is over."

He gave her a sudden smile which surprised Sarah by its warmth. She looked away quickly. He could turn that smile of his on and off at will, she told herself. It meant nothing.

"She can't live with you again," he went on. "That's hardly fair."

"I don't mind," Sarah said a little sharply. "If your solution is to send her away to school, I'd much rather have her with me. She'd be miserable at a boarding school."

"What about your own life?" he asked curiously. "Don't you miss your privacy, your freedom?"

"Sometimes," she confessed. "But not often. Ginny's happiness is very important to me."

"I know how hard you've worked to make your boutique a success," he told her. "And I know how hard you've worked on your clothing designs. I just don't understand why you're willing to give all that up for Ginny's sake. She's not even a relative. She's just some little kid you met in the park one day."

"I'm not giving up anything," she told him earnestly. For once he seemed to be in the mood to listen. If only she could get through to him. "I'm just making some adjustments in my life. I have discovered that my career isn't enough. There is something more to life than work—and that something is love. I've grown to love Ginny. Can you understand that?"

"Oh, I can understand that. But I can't understand your letting go of everything you've worked for."

"I won't be doing that," she said, leaning toward him as she tried to make her point. "I have no intention of letting everything go. I've worked far too hard for that. Besides, my career is still important to me. It's just not as important to me as it once was."

He gave her a thoughtful look. Sarah tried again. "You've helped me," she told him, thinking a little tact might come in handy at this moment. "If you hadn't forced my hand, so to speak, so that I practically *had* to come to the beach for the summer, I wouldn't have realized that my shop can get along without me. Do you know there hasn't been one emergency that somebody else hasn't been able to handle?"

He looked skeptical. "There must have been problems."

"Of course there have been problems. Some I've dealt with over the phone, some have been solved before I heard of them. I don't expect that to go on forever, but it does prove that I can take some time off, I can get away, without my entire business falling to pieces."

"I suppose you're telling me all this, hoping I'll realize that my business can do without me now and then, too?" he asked.

Though that was precisely what she was doing, Sarah was quick to deny it. She didn't want him to get the idea she was pushing him. "I don't know about your business," she said. "You'd have to make that decision for yourself. I'm just telling you that I thought I was indispensable, and I'm not."

"And I might discover the same thing, is that it?"

"You might," she said calmly. "You never know."

"As a matter of fact," he said, "I think you're probably wrong. I don't believe my business can function as it is without me there all the time. At least not without a major reorganization."

"Why not? Don't you hire people you can trust, people you can depend on?"

"Of course I do, but they're not used to working on their own."

Sarah was silent. She and David were talking as they never had before. She didn't know what to say next. She didn't want to start an argument—and this was a topic which was fraught with emotion. Certainly they had argued over it enough in the past.

"Don't you ever get tired of it?" she finally asked. "The constant travel, the demands on your time?"

"No," he said quickly, "never." His answer came so fast that it made Sarah wonder.

"I understand the challenge, the feeling you must get from meeting that challenge and the way you must feel when what you're working on is successful," she said slowly. She wanted him to know she understood. Perhaps then he would try to understand how she felt. "I just think there comes a time when you have to realize that people are important, too. And that they matter just as much as your work."

She held her breath. If he was going to get angry, this would be the time. It was possible she had said too much.

He shook his head but he didn't seem upset. She was grateful for that. If she made him angry now, it might undo all the good she hoped their conversation had accomplished.

"I'm not sure you're right," he said. "But I'm not sure you're wrong either."

She smiled to herself. Perhaps she was making some progress, after all.

"As a matter of fact," he went on, "I want Ginny to move out to Five Oaks when the summer is over."

At that Sarah's heart bounded. She was making progress. This was proof of it.

"She'll be delighted," Sarah told him. "I can't think of anything that would make her happier."

David shook his head. "I don't know. It might not work out. I'm going to try to give her the kind of home she needs but . . ." His voice trailed off.

Sarah's heart went out to him. David had suddenly become very human, and Sarah felt herself responding. This was the David she had come to love. "At least you're willing to try," she told him earnestly.

Again he shook his head. "It won't be easy." His voice changed slightly, and Sarah could hear his doubts. "I have meetings which last into the night and trips which come up suddenly. There will be times when Ginny is there alone with only the housekeeper for company. It may not work out at all."

"It will work out," Sarah told him. She put her hand on his arm. "It will work out if you want it to."

He gave her an enigmatic look. "I'm not even sure that I want it to. It means a complete change in my life-style. I'm not sure I'm cut out to be an uncle, let alone a substitute father."

Sarah felt a sudden chill, but she refused to be discouraged by his words. "I think you'll find it's worthwhile," she said.

He leaned back and gave her another warm smile. "We'll see. You do care a lot about Ginny, don't you?"

And about you too, she wanted to add. But she knew better than that. "Yes, I do care a great deal about her," she said instead. "She's a very special little girl."

"You're very special, too," he told her, capturing her hand.

Sarah would have withdrawn it, should have withdrawn it, but she was too bemused by the look in his eyes. The constraint between them was gone. David was again the man he had been during their first few days at the beach. He was once again the man she had fallen in love with . . . head over heels in love.

"The way you took Ginny in without expecting anything in return," he went on as he stroked her hand. "I know I misjudged your motives, but I've never met anyone quite like you before."

And she had never met anyone like him, she thought as she looked into his warm dark eyes. Cold and ruthless one minute, he could be warm and charming the next.

Careful, Sarah warned herself. David could change more quickly than anyone she had ever known. This mood of his would not last, and she would be right back where she started—unhappy and miserable.

He leaned forward, cupped her chin in his hand and gently brushed her lips with his. It was a gentle kiss, and it made Sarah's lips want to call his back to hers. She gave him a searching look but could find nothing in his face except a kind of lazy happiness. There was certainly no anger, no resentment, none of the things he had shown last night.

He slipped his arm around her and pulled her against him. Together they leaned back against the high dunes and watched the ocean as it moved in and out.

"The water is very quiet today, isn't it?" David asked softly. "Instead of crashing onto the beach it comes up almost gently."

"I'm not sure which I like best," Sarah told him. "It's so peaceful when it's like this, but I also like to see the power and force of the waves."

His arm tightened around her, and Sarah felt a surge of gladness around the region of her heart.

"What else do you like?" he wanted to know.

"Walking in the rain; driving through the countryside in the fall when the leaves are changing color; sitting in front of a roaring fire on a cold night," she said a little absently.

She wasn't paying too much attention to what they were saying. It was enough that they were sitting together in harmony with no one but themselves for miles and miles. Sarah felt as though a wish had come true. This was the David she had yearned for, the one she loved so desperately.

"Even though I had that investigation done on you," he was saying, "I really don't know much about you. But what I do know, I like."

He tilted her head back and looked deep into her eyes. Sarah felt as though she were floating, as though her body was being buoyantly and gently carried by currents of air. His eyes held hers as he slowly lowered his lips. Their lips touched lightly, and Sarah felt a pleasing warmth start to spread over her. The kiss was a warm and lazy one, calculated to start her heart beating quickly. And it did. Sarah felt her pulse speed up, just as she felt David slide a little lower on the sand.

He held her close, gently running his hand up and down her back. Sarah lay against him, letting her head rest on his chest. Beneath his shirt, she could hear the pounding of his heart. It was a firm steady sound, as comforting and as hypnotic as the sound of the ocean.

"Are you comfortable?" he asked.

"Very," she replied as she snuggled a little closer. Actually, this was her idea of heaven, but she wasn't going to say that.

"I enjoy the beach so much," he said, "that every time I'm here I wonder why I don't come more often." His hand found the place where her sweatshirt and slacks met and slipped beneath it to touch her bare skin.

Sarah felt a shock of surprise as his warm hand caressed the small of her back. She tried to sit up, but David held her tight.

"It's all right," he said softly. "There's nothing to worry about."

Reassured, she leaned back against him. It seemed he was right. There was nothing overtly sensuous in the touch of his hand. If anything, he was merely trailing his fingers across her back in an absentminded fashion. His mind seemed to be elsewhere. Sarah felt herself relax, and she began to enjoy the tingling sensations he caused. His mind might be elsewhere, but hers definitely was not.

"You should spend more time at the Gull's Nest," she told him dreamily. She didn't know when she had been more happy. "It agrees with you."

"You agree with me," he said as he claimed another kiss.

Under the influence of the slowly warming sun,

David's gently moving hands and the feel of his lips, Sarah felt a delicious languor steal over her. Her body grew pliant under his touch, and she let him lie her back on the sand. His lips moved to her closed eyes and her cheeks. Sarah lay quietly, barely breathing. She was almost afraid to move for fear she would break the spell and this David would once again disappear.

Carefully he brushed her dark hair away from her face. Sarah felt a bubble of happiness grow within her. At this moment, David was everything she had ever hoped for. He was gentle, yet masterful, and the feeling she got from his kisses was more than passion. The desire was there, but it was carefully controlled as if he didn't want to do anything to frighten her. Sarah wanted to lie in his arms forever.

His lips moved lightly across her face and back to her mouth. This time, as they possessed hers, there was more urgency to the kiss. Sarah felt her own lips part as his tongue probed skillfully and gently in her mouth. As her tongue touched his, her heart began to race, and a lethargy took control of her body.

David leaned over her, kissing her with a slow deliberateness which began to inflame her own feelings of passion. She had no idea what their kisses were doing to him, but they were setting her own body on fire. She began to tingle, and her breath came a little faster.

David's hand left her back and for a moment Sarah missed the feel of it on her bare skin. Then it moved across her stomach and down her leg. As his hand traveled down her thigh, Sarah stiffened for a second, then felt herself relax again. Slowly his hand moved back up, across the tight fabric of her khaki slacks to her waist. Gently his hand continued to slide upward, again under her shirt, producing new thrills of excitement.

When his fingers touched her bare nipple, Sarah felt

she would faint. She had been in such a hurry when she left the house that she had put on only a shirt and slacks. Nothing else. Though the fact that David had discovered she wore no underthings nearly made her blush, she was glad she had left them off.

Under the stimulus of David's fingers, Sarah felt her nipples harden. She moaned softly and, in response, David's hand closed firmly around her breast. She moaned again. She couldn't help it. Never had she felt such exquisite sensations, never had she imagined that the touch of a man's hand could be so sweet.

As he felt her desire grown, David's kisses became more possessive, more urgent. The movement of his hands became more feverish. Before she quite realized it, he had slipped her shirt over her head and carefully turned it into a pillow for her head.

Sarah felt a momentary urge to protect herself from his roving eyes, but it died as she saw the look on his face. He obviously found her beautiful, and her nipples began to grow even more taut as his eyes caressed her breasts. For a moment her breath caught in her throat, then she reached up and pulled him to her.

His lips met hers and the kiss, though fiery, was gentle. Slowly his lips moved down her neck, across her shoulders, toward her breasts. They moved slowly, so slowly that Sarah began to quiver before they closed over her nipples. Carefully, almost reverently, he kissed her breasts, letting his lips arouse her to a pitch she hadn't dreamed existed.

Sarah lay back in the sand, her heart racing and every nerve in her body crying out to him. One of her arms lay inert in the sand beside her while her other hand was caught in his thick dark hair. She caressed his head and neck lightly as he moved from one breast to the other.

In the dim corners of her mind, with what little power of thought she had left, Sarah knew this was an experience to be treasured. This was the kind of lovemaking normally to be found only in books. Though she could feel the strength of David's passion, it was obvious he was controlling it rather than letting it control him. She was grateful for his gentleness. It both pleased and touched her. And she was grateful, too, that he was taking his time, that he wasn't pushing her too quickly.

She felt no embarrassment at the fact that she was laying half-naked in the sand. Instead her great love for David seemed to envelop them both, increasing her own desire and, in turn, his.

As his lips moved back to hers and their tongues touched, Sarah could feel David's hands at the waistband of her slacks. He fumbled with the zipper for a moment, then checked his movements, raised his head and listened intently. Sarah didn't hear anything; she couldn't have heard anything over the pounding of her heart.

Impatiently she tried to pull him back to her, but he resisted. A moment later, he slipped the shirt down over her head and pulled it toward her waist. She stared at him wonderingly, the desire in her eyes plain for him to see.

Before she could speak, to ask him why, she heard the sound of voices, children's voices, from just over the sand dune. Only seconds later, five children, loaded down with shovels and buckets, passed by them on their way to the water. In a matter of moments they were followed by three adults.

Sarah felt completely disoriented, and she realized that if it hadn't been for David, she would have been caught half-dressed. But, thanks to him, by the time the children arrived, she was sitting up staring out at the ocean, and he was lounging a few feet away from her. Beyond a perfunctory look, the children ignored them, but to the adults, it looked as though they were enjoying nothing more than an early morning conversation. No one could have guessed at the tumult in her body.

"What time is it?" Sarah asked. She didn't look directly at David. She was still feeling a little dazed. The riotous desire in her body refused to die slowly. She could still feel his hands on her breasts, and it was with a great effort that she suppressed a shiver. She was also a little embarrassed. What was he thinking, she wondered. Was he as disappointed as she was or had her efforts at lovemaking merely amused him?

"I don't know," he said. "I was in such a hurry this morning that I left without my watch."

At the sound of his voice, Sarah stole a look at him. He was smiling at her in such a warm special way that her shyness disappeared. She smiled back. She wanted to throw back her head and laugh. Never had she felt so wonderful.

"We'd better get back to the house," she said. "Ginny is probably wondering what happened to us."

David jumped to his feet then extended a hand. Sarah put her hand in his and allowed him to pull her up. They stood close together for a moment, gazing into each other's eyes.

"You are beautiful," he told her softly. "Inside and out."

At that Sarah blushed a warm pink color. She remembered the feel of David's eyes on her bare skin. The caress of his eyes had been so intense that it was almost physical. She turned back toward the house, well aware that the pink in her cheeks was betraying her lack of sophistication in this area. As she turned she felt, rather than saw his grin. He dropped his arm over her shoulder, and together they walked back to the Gull's Nest.

As they ambled along, Sarah gloried in her feeling for David and the rapture they had shared. Never had she been happier, never had anyone been happier, she told herself as the sun shone down on them.

A doubt, cloudlike, floated across her mind. This morning had been so different from last night. Which one was the real David? No, she thought stubbornly, she wouldn't think of last night. She was determined to hold on to her happiness for as long as it would last.

Chapter Nine

"Super," Ginny cried after David told her that she would be moving out to Five Oaks at the end of the summer. "Does that mean I won't have to go back to that school you sent me to before I lived with Sarah?"

"That's exactly what it means," David said. He and Sarah had gotten back from their walk to find Ginny fixing herself some cold cereal.

Ginny let out a whoop of joy which was undoubtedly heard up and down the beach. She raced toward David, throwing herself at him with such force that he staggered backward slightly. Sarah could see that he was gratified by Ginny's response, but she also thought she saw some lingering doubts at the back of his eyes.

"What about Sarah?" Ginny asked him "Where will she live?"

"I'll live in my townhouse, of course," Sarah said hastily. "Where else would I live?"

"I wish you could live with us," Ginny said wistfully. "Don't you, Uncle David?"

157

David had such a strange expression on his face that Sarah would have laughed if she hadn't felt a sudden pain in the region of her heart. Living with them was just what she would like to do, but she knew it was impossible. David made no bones about the fact that he was still tied to his career. In having Ginny live with him, he would have to make some major sacrifices, some he admitted he wasn't sure he was ready to make. Another woman in his life would be impossible, Sarah thought miserably, even if he cared for her as much as she cared for him.

She forced herself to laugh. "I'll see lots of you," she promised Ginny. "You'll see."

She was very aware of David's silence as she spoke. He seemed to be looking anywhere but at her.

"I know, but . . ." Ginny began.

"You and I have disrupted Sarah's life enough as it is," David told her firmly. "I think it's time we let her get back to her own concerns."

His words hurt Sarah, all the more because of the moments they had just shared on the beach. Then it had seemed as though she meant something to him. Now it seemed as though he couldn't wait for the summer to be over to get rid of her. Sarah masked the pain in her eyes and bent over to give Ginny a kiss.

"Who wants breakfast?" she asked brightly. She wasn't going to let David see how much his words hurt her.

"French toast?" Ginny asked hopefully. She looked at her cold cereal distastefully.

"French toast it is," Sarah told her.

Resolutely she made the French toast, forcing herself to think of nothing but the task at hand. She tried desperately to recapture the feelings of happiness she had felt as she walked into the house and, by the end of breakfast, she had nearly succeeded. Most of her doubts had been pushed to the back of her mind.

David, too, seemed determined to restore the feeling

of intimacy between them, the feeling that had been shattered by Ginny's innocent questions. Sarah fell in with his mood easily. He had been so tender and gentle with her as they lay making love on the beach. Sarah wanted to remember that experience. Until David's mood changed again, she would live for the moment.

For the next few weeks, she managed to do just that. David stayed at the Gull's Nest and, though he spent a good part of each day on the telephone with people from his office, Sarah could see that he was really trying to fit Ginny into his life. She was delighted by that, of course, but she couldn't help wishing that there was some way she could fit into his life as well.

Hints of fall began appearing and it became obvious that summer was drawing to a close. For Sarah, the ending of summer had a bittersweet note to it.

These last few weeks with David had been wonderful. He remained the man she loved, and each day Sarah found her love for him had grown. Saying good-bye to him and Ginny at the end of the summer would come close to breaking her heart, and she knew it. Oh, she'd see Ginny, and occasionally David, on weekends, but never again would they be able to recapture the relaxed happiness of their weeks at the Gull's Nest.

But, Sarah thought as she tried to convince herself that all was working out for the best, there was a positive note to the end of the summer. Once she was back at her house in Georgetown, she would no longer have to endure the torture of being so close to David. She would not be constantly tempted to run her fingers through his hair or to simply touch him each time he walked by.

He had not sought her out since that early morning weeks before and that, too, was a kind of torture. Each day Sarah wondered if today would be the day he put his arms around her and drew her close.

She lived in a state of suspense. Whenever he came

close, she had to restrain herself from reaching out to him. Simply put, she wanted him. She wanted to feel the strength of his arms and the power of his lips. He wanted the same thing. She knew that. Though his hands did not caress her, his eyes did. They made his desire for her abundantly clear. Why, then, she asked herself, is he waiting? She also wondered what her response would be if he did take her in his arms. Twice before she had come close to giving herself to him. If there was a next time, what would she do?

As the days grew shorter, it appeared there would be no time to find out. Sarah was alternately disappointed and relieved. Though she yearned to love David as a woman loved a man, she knew the act of love, itself, would imply a commitment on her part . . . an implication David would reject.

So the weeks passed for Sarah in a haze of tortured uncertainty. Finally only one week remained. One more week, Sarah thought unhappily, and she would no longer be haunted by David's presence. She would be safe from him, still in possession of her body—if not her heart, for her heart had been given to him long ago.

Ginny's voice interrupted her thoughts. "Kathy asked me to stay the night with her," she said. "Do you think it will be all right with Uncle David?" She didn't sound very optimistic. Obviously she expected her uncle to say no.

"Will what be all right with me?" he asked as he came into the kitchen. As usual he had spent most of the morning on the phone with his office.

"If I stay all night with Kathy?" Ginny asked a little warily. She knew that her uncle did not like Kathy's father. "They're leaving in a couple of days, and this will be our last chance," she added as she saw David frown.

"I think it will be all right," he said finally.

"Really?" Ginny asked incredulously.

He nodded.

Sarah gave him a quick look. Like Ginny, she had expected him to say no. Then his glance caught hers, and Sarah felt something twist in the pit of her stomach as she realized what his decision meant. They would be alone, with no interruptions, for the entire night.

"I'll go tell her it's okay," Ginny said joyfully.

"Don't be gone long," Sarah said automatically. "Lunch is almost ready." Her eyes were still locked with David's. She couldn't seem to tear them away. She knew now why he had said yes, why he had agreed to let Ginny spend the night at the home of the man he considered an enemy.

David read her thoughts. As soon as the door slammed behind Ginny, he crossed the room and tilted Sarah's chin with his hand. The message in his eyes was unmistakable. It turned Sarah's bones to water. "I think we've earned a night to ourselves," he said softly, his eyes searching hers. "Don't you agree?"

Sarah couldn't answer. It didn't matter. He seemed to take her agreement as a matter of course. Slowly he leaned over and brushed his lips against hers. Sarah's eyes closed as she felt the heat of his mouth.

He pulled away, and she opened her eyes slowly. Her lips burned from their brief contact with his. She ran her tongue over them, trying to temper the heat. David watched her, desire suddenly alive in his face.

"We'll be able to finish something which should have been finished long ago."

His meaning was clear. Sarah leaned back against the counter for support. Again he teased her with a kiss. Though only their lips touched, Sarah felt her body burst into flames. She wanted a night of lovemaking as much as he did.

Outside, they heard Ginny's voice. Her knees trembling, Sarah turned back to the *salade niçoise* she was preparing. All through lunch she had to force herself to join in the conversation, to pay attention. Her mind was on the evening to come.

What should she do, she asked herself over and over. There was a measure of desperation in her question. She wanted David, wanted every part of him. She knew that. She also knew that her heartbreak would double if she allowed herself to fully taste the pleasures of his lovemaking. Already the idea of parting was agony to her. She'd feel that much worse if she loved him as completely with her body as she did with her mind. On the other hand, her memories, at least, would be sweet . . .

"Ken said he'd take Kathy and me to Rehoboth for pizza," Ginny was saying. "You don't mind, do you?"

"No," David answered. "We don't mind." His eyes lingered meaningfully on Sarah's face.

"What would you like for dinner?" Sarah asked him in a determinedly practical voice. She had to break through the sensuality of his glance.

"I'll take care of dinner," he told her.

"You can't fix anything but fish," Ginny scoffed. "I'll bet Sarah's sick of fish. I am. Why don't you have pizza with us?"

"Thanks anyway," David told her. "I have something a little more elegant in mind."

"I'm glad I'm not going to be here," Ginny said. "I'd rather have pizza." She gathered up a few dishes and took them into the kitchen.

Sarah took one look at David's face, picked up a plate and fled into the kitchen after her.

She stayed away from David as much as she could for the rest of the afternoon. The prospect of nightfall hung like a sword over her head. One moment she longed for the sun to go down, a moment later she hoped it would stay up forever. No matter how she felt, however, the hours marched inexorably on.

Eventually the heat of the day disappeared and night approached. Ginny packed her clothes in a small bag and happily said good-bye. Sarah watched her go, her feelings in turmoil. If only she were going, too, she couldn't help thinking. She turned to find David watching her with a look of appreciation in his eyes. She knew he was thinking of what would come later, after dinner. She was thinking about it, too. She hoped her embarrassment didn't show on her face.

"I'm in charge for the rest of the evening," he told her. "I want you to relax and enjoy yourself."

"I'll be glad to help you with dinner," she offered a little unsteadily. Something in his eyes was making her feel weak.

"Not tonight," he told her. "I'd rather you go upstairs, have a long bath and put on something appropriate. You know what I mean, something soft and sexy."

Sarah swallowed. "There's plenty of time for that. Why don't I help you a little before I go?" If she could keep things on a practical level, she was thinking, perhaps the seemingly inevitable would not happen.

He walked toward her and put his hands on her shoulders. Sarah wanted to turn and run. She also wanted to step forward into the comforting circle of his arms. She forced herself to stand still.

"Tonight is going to be a very special night—for both of us." His eyes probed hers deeply. "I don't want you to be hot and irritable from working in the kitchen." Slowly he drew her to him and held her gently. Sarah went willingly, and a moment later she was glad her head was hidden against his shoulder, because his next words made her blush.

"When you come down to dinner, I want you to be relaxed; I want your skin to be soft and silky to my touch. After dinner, when I kiss you, I want to know that your mind is on me and not on the dinner dishes." There was a hint of laughter in his voice. He tilted her head up so that he could kiss her. It was a lingering kiss, and it conveyed the sense of promise he meant it to.

"I could make love to you here and now," he whispered into her ear as her arms unwittingly wrapped around his neck. "But I won't. I want tonight to be memorable for both of us."

Gently he removed her arms from his neck. She didn't look at him. She couldn't.

"I'll call you when dinner is ready," he said. "Until then, you have nothing to worry about, nothing to think about, but what's going to happen this evening."

Sarah turned and walked out of the kitchen and up the stairs to her room in a daze. He didn't realize it, but that was all she had thought about for the last few weeks.

Mechanically, she ran warm water into the bathtub, splashing in perfumed bath salts which filled the air with scent. She soaked long and languorously in the tub, trying to decide how she was going to act that evening. David took their lovemaking as a given but, though her body ached for him, she wasn't quite that far along. What was she going to do? she asked herself over and over again. What should she do? She had just finished sweeping her hair on the top of her head when there was a soft rapping at her door.

"Dinner's ready whenever you are," David called from the hall.

"I'll be down in just a few moments," she said, trying to keep her voice steady. Her heart was suddenly pounding.

"I'll be waiting," he answered.

Sarah understood precisely what he meant. With trembling hands, she pulled a long, lilac-colored strapless dress over her head. The dress was made of a thin jersey which stretched over her breasts and hugged her waist before flaring slightly into a graceful skirt. The color of the dress deepened her eyes, making them soft and velvety looking.

Sarah stared at herself in the mirror. She barely recognized herself—not because she looked so different, but because she was looking at a woman who was about to go downstairs and have dinner with the man who was soon to be her lover.

As Sarah gazed at herself, she had the feeling that she was two people. A part of her was going eagerly to David, the other part of her was holding back, reluctantly afraid of being hurt.

Did she really have the nerve to go downstairs? she asked herself. Could she show herself in this dress which covered her body but left nothing to the imagination to a man who had only one thing in mind?

Before she quite realized it, she was standing in the living room. David was pouring wine into two wineglasses, but he stopped as he saw her. His eyebrows rose, and his breath drew in swiftly. Sarah began to tremble. Though she tried, she couldn't make herself walk forward. She stayed where she was and let his eyes devour her.

"You're breathtaking," he told her softly. He crossed the room and ran his hands slowly up and down her bare shoulders and arms.

Sarah shivered as he touched her. Trustingly she lifted her lips, hoping he would kiss her. His eyes darkened as he stared down at her, but instead of kissing her, he took her arm and led her over to the sofa.

"I've poured you some wine," he told her. Carefully, as though she were something fragile and very precious, he seated her. Only after he had made sure she was comfortable did he hand her a glass with white wine in it.

Sarah took it and held it tightly in her hands. David was making her feel not only desired, he was making her feel cherished. With his own glass he lightly touched hers. It made a ringing sound.

"To tonight," he said. "A night worth the wait."

Sarah took a big sip, more because she needed it to steady her nerves, than in response to his toast.

"Don't drink too much," he cautioned her. "I don't want your senses to be jaded by alcohol. I want you to feel everything that happens." David set his own glass on the table and leaned toward her.

"You're so far away," he murmured. Gently he pulled her closer. Sarah clenched the wineglass as she felt herself incline against him. The coldness of the glass was helping her maintain a sense of reality.

Her senses careened suddenly, however, when David began nibbling at her neck. Slowly and lazily his mouth began moving over the sensitive skin. Sarah felt little goose bumps rise all over her body, and she began to quiver.

"You're not nervous, are you?" he asked teasingly. He removed the wineglass from her hands and pressed her body against his. His hands moved slowly down her back and over her rounded bottom. "Are you?" he asked again. It was almost as though he sensed her fear.

"A little," she confessed. Her voice was so soft it was almost a whisper. To herself, she acknowledged that she was more than nervous, she was terrified. Terrified of giving herself to him, terrified of not giving herself to him.

"There's no reason to be," he told her. His lips lit on her eyelids, her cheeks, her forehead. "We both know it's going to be a very special night. I'm going to do everything I can to make it a memorable one." He stood and pulled her to her feet. "But first, dinner."

With one arm draped lightly around her shoulders, he led her to the dinner table. It was alight with candles, and there was soft music in the background. Sarah slid into the chair he held for her, grateful to be sitting. Her legs were weak with anticipation and fear.

No one could ever want more romance than this, she thought. As she looked at David in the candlelight, her heart melted. He was so handsome, so virile, and the look in his eyes told her that, for the moment anyway, she was the most desirable woman in the world.

Was it only last spring that she had wished for excitement and glamour in her life? she asked herself. Now she had both, and she would be a fool not to enjoy them for as long as they lasted. She'd let tomorrow take care of itself, she decided. It was madness, she knew that. But only a woman made of stone would have been able to resist David and all he was offering. And she, very definitely, was not made of stone.

A man in a white jacket suddenly appeared from the kitchen. He was carrying a tray which held two small bowls of lobster bisque. He put the bowls down in front of them and, after pouring their wine, disappeared as silently as he had come. Sarah looked at David in complete surprise.

"He's a waiter from a restaurant in Rehoboth. I asked the owner if he would mind preparing the food, then sending someone to serve it."

"And to think that I supposed you were down here slaving over a hot stove," Sarah said, finding her tongue.

He looked at her in mock horror. "Ginny's right," he said. "The only thing I can cook is fish. It's good, but I didn't think it would be appropriate for tonight."

"What were you doing then?" she asked, more to make conversation than because she really wanted to know. She tasted the bisque. It was delicious, though she really didn't feel like eating. Her stomach was so full of butterflies there was no room for food.

"Actually, I was on the phone with my office."

Reality intruded for a moment. What else would he have been doing, Sarah asked herself wryly. Even though he was physically absent from his office, he was frequently there mentally. At the very least, he seemed tied to the telephone.

Sarah stared at the man sitting across from her. Though he had arranged for this romantic dinner, though his lips and hands were warm, though she loved him both passionately and tenderly, she had to remem-

ber that his career came first. Next week he would
return to that career, saying good-bye to her without a
second thought. She was a diversion, a way of passing
time while he was away from his first love, his only
love, his job. Resolutely, Sarah pushed the thought
away. She was going to enjoy the evening, no matter
what the consequences.

The waiter removed her barely touched bowl of soup
and put a plate in its place. On the plate was crab
imperial and an assortment of vegetables, decoratively
arranged. After he had served David, he wished them
bon appetit and returned to the kitchen. A moment
later, Sarah heard the kitchen door close softly. They
were alone.

"I told him I'd take care of dessert myself," David
told her. His eyes lingered on her face with such
meaning that Sarah stared down at her food without
really seeing it.

"Who will clean up?" she asked.

"You're not to worry about that. Someone will be
over early tomorrow morning to clean up and take the
dishes back to the restaurant. I said you would have
nothing to do but enjoy tonight, and I meant it."

The meal passed mostly in silence. Sarah could think
of nothing to say, to her it seemed as though there was
nothing to say. She toyed with her food. The butterflies
in her stomach made eating difficult, if not impossible.
Even her wine went largely untasted. She tried to sip at
it, thinking it would help her relax, but she really didn't
want it.

Finally the meal was over. David helped her up, and
Sarah thought he was going to kiss her. She was
relieved when he didn't. Despite her decision to take
each moment as it came and to let tomorrow take care
of itself, she felt a twinge of panic as she realized that
now nothing stood between them and David's promise
of a night to remember.

"I think I'll go freshen up," she said as her panic

intensified. She backed away from him, then practically ran out of the room.

Alone in her bedroom she pressed icy hands to her hot face. Except for her hands, her entire body felt feverish. She had made her decision, she told herself over and over. Why then, did she feel such trepidation? Why, then, was she so nervous?

Sarah stepped out on the balcony, hoping the gentle winds off the ocean would cool her body. She closed her eyes, letting the breeze caress her.

"I thought we'd have dessert in my room," David said softly at her elbow. He had come onto the balcony from his room. Though she hadn't heard him as he walked toward her, Sarah wasn't surprised by his presence.

"I have some champagne and French pastries waiting for us," he said, drawing her toward the doors leading to his room.

Sarah allowed him to lead her inside. She was beginning to feel a little dazed by the intensity of her emotions—but whether those emotions were fear or desire, she no longer knew. She only knew that resisting him seemed futile. Worse than that, it seemed foolish.

Sarah perched on the edge of the loveseat across from his bed and stared around the room. She hadn't seen it before. She had purposely avoided it, sending Ginny to do whatever cleaning was necessary. She was afraid it would remind her too much of David and the times she had been in his arms. She was also afraid it would remind her of the other women he had brought to the Gull's Nest.

Now she noticed little but the large bed. It had been turned back invitingly, and there were plump pillows waiting to be used. Sarah stared at it. In a few moments, she thought, the two of them would be lying there, arms and legs entwined, their lips pressed together. The thought made her heart turn over.

There was a popping sound·as David opened the champagne. He poured it into a tall, fluted glass and handed it to her. After he had poured one for himself, he sat down beside her and held up the tray of pastries for her to inspect.

She shook her head. "No, thank you," she said. Her voice was almost a whisper. "I couldn't eat anything." Something seemed to have happened to her breathing.

"I don't want any either," he said. "We have more important things to do."

Sarah sipped at her champagne, growing more and more nervous. If only the evening hadn't been so deliberately planned, she thought. Twice before she had come close to giving herself to him. Twice before she would have given herself to him, but for unwanted and unwelcome interruptions. Now she would have welcomed an interruption. Those other times had been spontaneous and somehow right. But this, this was cold-blooded and somehow wrong.

David took her glass and pulled her close. For a few moments Sarah felt herself respond to his hands and lips. Why not, she told herself. This was what she wanted. She felt the world begin to slip away as he caressed her sensuously.

He got up to dim the lights and her eyes opened reluctantly. The first thing she saw was the bed. It seemed to fill the room. Once the lights had been lowered, David sat down on it and motioned for her to join him.

Obediently she got to her feet and walked slowly toward him. His eyes traveled over her as she moved, making her breasts swell and her nipples harden. When she reached him, he took her in his arms and gently pulled her down beside him. His hands ran feverishly down her body and again Sarah felt herself respond. She was beginning to think it would be wrong to resist him. Certainly only a small part of her wanted to resist. The rest of her body was clamoring to possess . . . to be possessed. She felt herself sinking deeper and deeper into the softness of the bed. If only she could bury that one protesting part of her, there would be nothing in the world but David and his soft, comfortable bed.

The bed! A sudden thought penetrated the velvety blackness which was beginning to envelop her. How many women had he brought to this bed? It didn't really matter, except for one thing. She didn't want to join their numbers. She knew now she couldn't. The price was too high. To love him this way, sweet though it might be, would make their parting doubly painful. And that parting was only a week away.

Sarah suddenly knew a week spent enjoying the pleasures of David's lovemaking would not be enough . . . not nearly enough. In the long run she'd be better off to leave him now, while she still could.

"I can't," she thought in anguish. The thought hit her like a blow.

"Can't what?" David asked. His voice was drugged with passion.

Sarah hadn't realized she had spoken aloud. She would have liked to recall the words, but she knew she couldn't.

"I can't go through with this," she said. Her voice was trembling and tears filled her eyes. She slipped out of his arms before he could stop her and made her way to the door. She could barely see for the tears which were blinding her. She was halfway across the room when his voice stopped her.

"Where are you going?"

He sounded so bewildered that she knew she had to give him some kind of explanation. But what could she say? She blinked back her tears and turned to face him.

"I'm going to my room," she said quietly.

"Why?" His voice was sharper. "What's wrong?"

"This whole thing is wrong." She gestured around her. "I'm sorry, I just can't."

"I don't understand." The anger was growing in his voice. "You've been willing before. What makes this time so different?"

She didn't blame him for being angry. She hadn't given him much of an explanation. She couldn't. How could she tell him that she loved him too much to make love to him? A man like David de Courcey would never understand that.

David got to his feet and stared at her, waiting for an answer. Sarah felt her body tense. If he took a step toward her, she knew she'd have to turn and run.

"Those other times *were* different," she said falteringly. "They were more spontaneous. Tonight was so planned, so cold-blooded."

"What's wrong with that?" His voice took on a note of disdain. "You're not a little girl anymore, Sarah. Don't act like one."

"You're right," she said, making her voice cold. "I'm not a little girl. I have the right to make my own decisions. And I've decided that I'm going to my room . . . alone," she added pointedly. That, she hoped, would let him know once and for all that her decision could not be changed.

"Not without an explanation," he rapped out.

He took a step toward her. Sarah jumped and started to back toward the door.

"Don't be ridiculous," he said scornfully. "I'm not going to touch you." His eyes flashed angrily. "I've never had to plead with a woman I wanted, and I won't start with you."

Sarah felt the blood drain from her face. This was what she had been afraid of—of being put in the same category as all the other women who had passed in and out of his life. She was suddenly glad she had pulled away.

"Still, after the way you've behaved before, I think I deserve an explanation and you still haven't given me one." His eyes traveled slowly over her body. "Do you remember that morning on the beach?" In his voice Sarah could hear anger, and confusion. "If it hadn't been for those kids and their parents, we would have become lovers then."

Sarah's face flamed. He was right.

"I still don't understand what makes tonight so different."

Sarah shook her head. "I can't explain it," she said miserably.

"Why don't you try?"

She stared at him speechlessly. She could think of nothing to say. The truth was out of the question. Why put a weapon like the knowledge of her love in his hands? He would be amused to hear she loved him, he might even be touched. But that wouldn't alter the fact that he loved not her, but his career. And, perhaps without even realizing it, she was sure he would take advantage of her feelings for him. Before she knew it, she would be in his arms again, and she had to avoid that at all costs. No, she'd be better off telling him nothing and keeping her pride intact.

"I'm waiting." His face was glacial.

Sarah felt her dignity slipping away. She had to get out of that room before she broke down. She couldn't stand the way he was looking at her. She could actually feel her heart breaking.

"I'm sorry," she said unsteadily. He'd never know just how sorry she was. "There's nothing I can say that would make you understand. Let's just say I've changed my mind and leave it at that."

She turned slowly and a little unwillingly. She had taken a few steps toward the door when he again stopped her.

"Sarah!" There was a commanding note to his voice and also a faintly ominous one.

This time she didn't turn to face him. She couldn't

stop the tears from spilling down her cheeks, but she could keep him from seeing them. She had no wish to advertise her weakness.

"If you walk out that door, there won't be a second chance." His voice was quiet, but Sarah could hear the implacable anger in it.

She didn't answer. Instead, she forced her feet to take her to the door. With each step she took, the force of David's personality seemed stronger and stronger. It took every ounce of willpower she possessed not to turn and run back to him.

There was a cold silence behind her as she reached the door. David said nothing, but Sarah was aware of his eyes on her back. She jerked open the door and stepped into the hall. Quietly, she pulled the door shut behind her and leaned against it for a moment. The walk away from David had sapped her strength. It wasn't the physical act of walking out the door that drained her of all her energy, but the struggle within herself as she forced herself forward.

Inside the room she heard David suddenly swear. A second later she heard what sounded like a dish being hurled against the wall. The sounds gave her new energy, and she ran down the hall to her room where she flung herself down on her bed and sobbed out all her misery and frustration.

When she could cry no longer, she yanked off the lavender gown and threw it, and all her clothes, in a suitcase. Her fling with romance and excitement was over. When morning came, she was going back to Washington. Back to her career and her empty townhouse. Back where she belonged.

Chapter Ten

"You're up early," Ken said.

Sarah was standing by the front door of his house shivering a little from the cool morning air. She had knocked tentatively, not sure if anyone would be awake.

Ken was right. It was early. The sun was just beginning to fill the sky. Early or not, nothing would keep her in that house with David another minute.

"Is anything wrong?" Ken shot a look at her face, then looked away quickly.

Sarah knew her eyes were still red from all the tears she had shed. She just hoped Ken wouldn't be able to guess the cause.

"No, nothing's wrong," she told him. "At least nothing too serious. I've got to get back to Washington —there's an emergency at my shop." That was to be her excuse for leaving. David, of course, would know it wasn't true, but she wasn't using it out of concern for him. It was Ginny's feelings she wanted to spare.

"Is Ginny up yet?" she asked. "I'd like to see her before I go."

"She and Kathy were sound asleep a few minutes ago. Why don't you go on upstairs and wake her?"

Sarah started to refuse. She hated the idea of waking Ginny. But she disliked the idea of leaving without saying good-bye even more. Upstairs, in the room Ginny and Kathy were sharing, Sarah shook Ginny gently.

"Ginny, honey, it's me, Sarah." She spoke in a whisper.

Ginny stirred restlessly, then opened her eyes and rubbed them. "What are you doing here?"

"I'm sorry to wake you, but I've got to go back to Washington."

"You do?"

Sarah brushed the hair from Ginny's face. She was glad to see that Ginny seemed more surprised than upset. An emotional parting with Ginny would have undone her completely.

"I wanted to see you before I left."

"When will you be back?"

"I don't know that I will be back," Sarah told her. "There's a problem with my fall line of clothes, and I'm going to have to straighten it out. It may take days."

Ginny's face fell.

"You'll only be here a few more days yourself," Sarah reminded her. "Then you'll be going to Five Oaks with your uncle."

"But if you don't come back to the Gull's Nest, when will I see you again?"

Sarah hugged her tightly for a moment. "You'll see me the minute you get settled at Five Oaks. I promise. I'll come see you or you can come see me."

The promise was as much for her own sake as it was for Ginny's. She had come to love Ginny, and it hurt to be leaving her. Sarah knew that her relationship with Ginny could never be the same as it was when Ginny was living with her. And she knew that she would miss that. For a moment she almost regretted bringing Ginny and David together. It left her out in the cold.

"I want to see you before then," Ginny objected.

"I'll try to come back before you leave the beach," Sarah said. "I don't like saying good-bye like this either."

She crossed her fingers guiltily as she spoke. She had no intention of returning to the Gull's Nest—ever. It held too many memories for her. Some were happy but most were sad, even heartbreaking.

"But in case I don't manage to get back here, I want you to promise to call me as soon as you get to Five Oaks," she told Ginny firmly. "Is it a deal?"

Ginny smiled at her. "It's a deal."

Sarah was relieved. At least she was leaving Ginny in a good frame of mind. She wouldn't have to worry about her as she drove back to Washington.

"Could you do one thing for me?" Sarah asked before she left. "Tell your uncle I had to go back to town. He'll understand."

"Okay," Ginny nodded.

Sarah gave her another swift hug and a kiss. "Now you lie down and try to go back to sleep. It's not time to wake up for a couple more hours."

Obediently, Ginny put her head back on the pillow. Sarah smoothed the hair back from her eyes, then turned and quickly left the room.

She slipped out of the house without saying good-bye to Ken. She didn't think she could face another good-bye, not after the wrenching one she had just experienced. Before anyone or anything could stop her, she got in her car and drove off hurriedly.

She shouldn't have gone to the beach with them, she told herself, as she sped inland. The moment she had said she would go, she had also set herself up for the kind of misery she was experiencing now. Everything about the beach, from the skimpy clothes to the air of relaxation, was conducive to sex. Little wonder David had fallen prey to the atmosphere.

Her feelings for him made sex impossible. Sarah wanted, and needed, more. Though David kindled emotions in her she did not know existed, her love was too strong to be sated by a purely physical relationship. David's feelings were more shallow. An affair was all he wanted. He had never pretended otherwise.

At least, she thought with a sigh, she could tell herself that Ginny and David would not have become something close to a family without her help. That was some consolation.

The rest of the way home she made her mind blank. She could change nothing; there was no good to be found in trying. She pulled in front of her townhouse, grateful that she had her career. It wasn't much of a substitute for David and Ginny, but it was all she had. She collected her luggage and carried it inside. It was barely nine o'clock. The shop wouldn't open for another hour and that would give her forty-five minutes or so before she had to answer any questions about why she had returned early.

Two hours later, Sarah was back at work. But for the ache in her heart, the summer might not have taken place. She caught a glimpse of herself in the mirror. She was tanned and a little tired-looking but those were the only indications that she had been away for the summer. In her pale blue linen skirt and blouse, she looked crisp and professional. She was sure no one coming through the door could see the sadness in her eyes.

The morning wore on. Sarah began to have the feeling she had never been away. She talked to customers, solved a couple of minor problems and tried to ignore the pain in her soul. The lunch hour rush was just beginning, and Sarah looked at the people in her shop with satisfaction. There was no denying that business was good. She might not be any good at the art of love, but she certainly knew what she was doing when it came to designing clothes. Her assistant, too, she noted, was an asset to the shop. She handled the customers almost as well as Sarah did, herself.

"No, this skirt doesn't come in plum. But I can have it made up for you if you like," Sarah was saying to one of the women as she heard the door to her shop open and close softly. She wouldn't have paid any attention if it hadn't been for a sudden lull in conversation that accompanied the closing of the door. The silence lasted only a few seconds, then the women were all talking at once. Sarah turned to see what the problem was.

It was David. He stood just inside the door, dressed in his old, faded cut-off jeans and a T-shirt. He looked as though he had just come from the beach, as Sarah knew he had. His hair was tousled, and the fact that he was running his long, supple fingers through it didn't help the way it looked. In his other hand, a rectangular package wrapped in brown paper dangled from a string.

Even as Sarah felt her heart leap at the sight of him, then fall as she realized she would have to face him again, she noticed the glances he was getting from the other women. He looked completely out of place in the elegant, feminine atmosphere of Sarah's shop, but no one seemed to mind in the least. Instead the women were gazing at him speculatively, and Sarah could see that one or two of them were quietly discussing him as they looked.

What is he doing here? she asked herself frantically. What more can there be to say?

David scanned the room of women and located her quickly. Their eyes met. Bitter anguish washed over her. She wanted David out of her life. Last night had been almost unbearable. Another night of the same pain would kill her. With his eyes trained on Sarah, David walked purposefully across the room. The women in his way moved aside. The shop was quiet again as everyone watched to see what he would do.

Sarah watched him too, unhappiness and fear alive in her eyes.

David took her by the arm and without a word steered her out of her shop into the small sitting room in the back of the house. Sarah signalled to her assistant to take over.

As the door closed behind them, Sarah could hear the excited hum of conversation pick up. "That's David de Courcey," she heard one woman say. "Isn't he marvelous-looking? Did you see those legs?"

Sarah wrenched her arm away. "What are you doing here?" she asked angrily. "Can't you see how busy I am?"

"We have to talk," he said. His voice was low.

"There's nothing to say," Sarah told him. "We said everything last . . ." She stopped as she saw the look in his eyes. He was as unhappy as she was. Caught up in her own pain, she hadn't noticed his.

"What is it?" she asked sharply. "Is something wrong with Ginny?"

He made an impatient gesture. "It isn't Ginny I want to talk about. It's us."

"There is no us," Sarah said dully. Now that she knew Ginny was all right she couldn't imagine what he had to talk about. She just wanted him to go. She sank down on a chair near the small, marble fireplace and looked up at him with eyes which implored him not to hurt her anymore.

"You told me last night that there would be no second chance." She pulled her eyes away and tried to rally her forces. "And even if there were, I wouldn't take it."

"I was a fool," David said simply. "I couldn't see what had been staring me in the face for weeks."

He knelt down in front of her and laid the package he was holding in her lap. "This is for you."

"I can't accept anything from you," Sarah protested tiredly. Surely he had realized by now that he couldn't buy her. She tried to give it back to him, but he wouldn't take it.

"Open it," he said softly. "I won't force you to keep it if you don't want it."

Reluctantly, Sarah untied the string and removed the brown paper wrapping. Underneath the paper was a long, rectangular box. Sarah lifted the lid and gasped when she saw what was inside. It was her fish, their fish . . . the one she and David had caught together that morning last June. It had been stuffed and mounted on an oval piece of shiny wood. Below the fish was a small, brass plate engraved with her name and the date she had caught it.

"I'd forgotten all about it," Sarah said softly. Tears filled her eyes as she remembered the happiness she had felt that morning as she stood in David's arms. She remembered, too, the excitement of catching the fish and her exuberance as she had walked back to the cottage. It seemed like a very long time ago.

"I was going to give it to you last night," David told her.

Sarah suddenly became aware that he was still kneeling in front of her. Her heart urged her to reach out to him while her mind wanted him to leave. She could think of nothing to say.

"Do you like it?" he asked.

"Yes," she said. "Very much. Thank you for bringing it to me." She tried to get up, but she couldn't without touching him—and he apparently had no intention of moving. She shrank back in her chair, trying to get as far away from him as possible. She didn't look up. Instead, she kept her eyes on the fish.

He suddenly swore softly to himself. "This isn't the way it's supposed to be," he muttered. In a sweeping motion, he put the fish on the floor and took Sarah into his arms.

She stiffened but her words of protest were cut off by his lips. It was a gentle kiss. David's lips were warm and persuasive, and Sarah stopped thinking about anything at all once they touched hers. She loved him so much. He lifted his lips and gave her a warm grin.

"That's better," he told her. Effortlessly he lifted her out of her chair and placed her on the loveseat close to him.

Sarah was too surprised, and if truth be told, too bemused by his kiss to protest. After all, this was where she wanted to be. Why fight it? She let him kiss her again, let the sensuous stillness envelop her.

As if he sensed her acquiescence, David began moving his hands down her body. Sarah knew she had to resist. She knew she had to pull back. Just a few moments more, she promised herself. She felt so at home in his arms that it caused her physical pain to tear herself away. She wanted to enjoy the feel of his arms and lips a little longer before she deprived herself of them.

David's tongue teased her lips and they parted slightly. Lightly his tongue caressed the inside of her mouth. Sarah felt her breath start to come a little faster, just as her heart began to beat more rapidly. For a few seconds she melted against him and let her arms curl around his neck. Much as she enjoyed the feel of his body against hers, she knew the time was coming when she would have to pull away.

"Why did you come back to Washington?" David asked. "Why did you leave us?"

At the sound of the hurt in his voice, Sarah opened her eyes and looked into his face. She saw desire, of course, but she also saw something else. Something that took her breath away. Could it be that . . . Her common sense asserted itself. Don't be ridiculous, it said. She started to speak, but David laid a finger across her lips, stopping her.

"It's time for the truth," he told her softly.

Sarah began to squirm away. She didn't want to tell

the truth. The truth was why she had run from his room last night and run from his house this morning.

David held her tight. "The truth," he repeated.

Sarah stared up at him, then nodded wordlessly. Perhaps the truth would be best. At least then she would be free of him. He would not want her around once he learned of her love for him. That would be too cramping, too restricting. It would interfere with his career.

"All right," she agreed. She pulled away from him and leaned against the corner of the loveseat. "But I can't talk or think clearly when you're holding me."

"Neither can I," he confessed. "Perhaps that's been part of my problem."

Sarah looked at him questioningly as he again ran his fingers through his dark hair.

"Maybe I'd better begin at the beginning," he said hesitantly.

Sarah nodded encouragingly. If she didn't know better, she'd say that David was actually nervous. She laughed at herself for even thinking such a thing but still . . .

"When I first met you," he began, "I couldn't believe that anyone with your talents and ambition would put her work aside to help an unhappy little girl. Naturally I thought you were after something." He grinned wryly. "Do you remember telling me that my experiences in life must have been warping?"

"I should never have said that to you," Sarah told him.

He shrugged. "You were right. Until I met you, all the women in my life were after something. Money, a job in my company; some were even after marriage."

There was a silence which Sarah made no effort to break. There was something in his face that she couldn't quite believe. Hope began to bubble up inside her.

"You weren't like that," he went on finally. "I

couldn't understand why. I still don't understand it," he confessed ruefully. "I'm just glad you're the way you are."

Sarah stared at him. He was gazing at her seriously, but at the back of his eyes she could see an emotion she had never hoped to find there. Hope grew.

"I've watched you with Ginny; I've seen how you care for her. As I watched you put a little girl's happiness before your own ambitions, it began to occur to me that I could do the same thing."

"You can," Sarah said softly, thinking of Ginny. "I know you'll be glad you did. Ginny will . . ."

"At this moment it isn't Ginny I'm thinking of. It's you."

Sarah all but stopped breathing as he talked.

"You've taught me how to love. By watching you, I've learned what things in life are really important."

He took her tightly clenched hand in his and stroked it. Sarah felt her fingers respond. Slowly they relaxed.

"I want the three of us to be a family," he told her. There was a fearful eagerness in his eyes. It was as though he were afraid Sarah might not want the same thing he wanted.

"If this is some kind of a game," she began unsteadily. If this was a trick to get her in bed with him, she knew the pain would be too much to bear.

"A trick?" He sounded genuinely shocked, and his eyes grew earnest. "I love you. I've loved you for weeks, now. I've just been too blind to see it. If I hadn't been so afraid of facing my feelings, this would have been settled long ago."

Sarah heard the three words she had never expected, never even dared to dream of uttering. She heard no more.

"Say it again," she whispered. She was afraid to believe him.

"What?" He looked startled, then his face softened

into a warm smile. "I love you," he said, cupping her chin with his hand. He leaned over and kissed her with a tenderness which brought tears to her eyes. "I love you," he repeated. Gentle kisses touched her cheeks, her forehead, the quivering lids of her eyes. "I love you," he murmured as his lips returned to hers in a deeply satisfying kiss.

"And I love you, too," Sarah told him when her lips were once again free. "I think I've always loved you."

"Always?" He gave her a teasing glance.

"Since the beginning of time," she answered seriously. "I feel as though I've waited all my life to find you."

"I feel exactly the same way," he said with a seriousness which matched her own.

"Last night," Sarah began hesitatingly. "Last night I . . ."

He silenced her with another kiss. "Last night I was ten times a fool," he said harshly. "I was so caught up in what I wanted that I didn't stop to think that it might not be right for you. Instead of laying down the law, I should have talked to you and tried to discover what was wrong. Can you forgive me?"

"There's nothing to forgive," she said, tracing his face with her finger. "Last night was my fault."

"No, the fault was mine." David captured her hand and kissed it. "This morning, when I discovered you had gone, I was almost frantic. I knew I had driven you away. The only thing I could think to do was to come after you and straighten things out."

"I'm glad you did." Sarah left her corner of the loveseat and snuggled up against him. She knew there were things, practical things, they should discuss, but she was too happy to do anything but lean against him and delight in his love. Practical things could wait.

"Does that mean you'll go back to the Gull's Nest with me?"

"I just got here," she protested, though she knew

there was nothing she wanted more than to be with David . . . at the Gull's Nest or wherever he happened to be. "What will my assistant think if I turn around and leave?"

"She's had the whole summer to learn how to get along without you. It's a good thing, too. Now you won't have to break in anyone new before the wedding."

"The wedding?" she echoed blissfully.

"Of course. Do you want a small one or a large one?"

"Small," she replied. "Very small."

"That's my idea, too," he said approvingly. "The sooner the better. How does tomorrow or the next day sound?"

"It sounds wonderful." Sarah laughed out of sheer joy, then her voice grew sober. "There's only one problem." She sat up and pulled back a little. It was impossible for her to think with David's hands moving up and down her body.

"What is it?"

"Your job."

He grimaced.

Sarah looked at him doubtfully. "If the three of us are going to be a family, you'll have to delegate some of your responsibilities."

"You're right," he said. "I know you're right. That's just what I've been trying to do the past few weeks."

"I know you have. I just want you to realize that it won't be easy. Your career is the most important thing in your life."

"Was," he corrected. "It was the most important thing in my life."

Sarah gazed into his eyes and was reassured by what she saw there.

Gently he smoothed back her hair. "Of course it won't be easy. Few truly worthwhile things are. But

we'll manage. I'll have you to help me." The seriousness disappeared from his voice and eyes. "Now come
over here. Before we go back to the beach, I want to do
a little celebrating—just the two of us."

He gathered Sarah up in his arms and pressed her
close. She slipped her arms around his neck as he
caressed her gently. His mouth nuzzled her neck,
producing shivers up and down her spine. In a matter of
minutes, her body began responding to his touch. Her
breath came faster and her heart pounded with love.
She wriggled against him, wanting to be as close to him
as possible. Being in his arms felt so right.

"Sarah," he whispered in her ear, "I love you more
than I can tell you."

"And I love you," she whispered back.

"There's just one thing I want to know." He pulled
back slightly. "What happened last night? Did I do
something to hurt you? To frighten you?"

Sarah felt her cheeks turn pink. She buried her head
in David's shoulder.

"Tell me what it was so I won't do it again."

"It was nothing like that," Sarah's voice faltered,
then stopped.

"What was it, then?" His voice was gently insistent.
"I thought you wanted me as much as I wanted you."

"I did," she said confusedly. "I do. But . . ." Again
her voice died away.

He looked at her questioningly.

"Don't you understand?" she burst out. "I've
never . . ." She couldn't finish the sentence.

David tilted her head back and probed her eyes with
his own. "Do you mean to tell me that you're a virgin?"
There was amazement in his voice. "In this day and
age?"

She nodded wordlessly. The pink in her cheeks
deepened. "Do you still want me?"

"Do I still want you?" he asked incredulously.

"You're a treasure. I want you, I love you and I promise to cherish you." There was a warm laughter in his voice which was combined with a contentment so rich and so obvious that Sarah felt her world could contain no more happiness. "Don't worry. We'll have that night to remember yet," he promised her. "That night and many more."

Fall in love again for the first time
every time you read a Silhouette Romance novel.

If you enjoyed this book, and you're ready to be carried away by more tender romance...get 4 romance novels FREE when you become a Silhouette Romance home subscriber.

Act now and we'll send you four touching Silhouette Romance novels. They're our gift to introduce you to our convenient home subscription service. Every month, we'll send you six new Silhouette Romance books. Look them over for 15 days. If you keep them, pay just $11.70 for all six. Or return them at no charge.

We'll mail your books to you two full months *before they are available anywhere else.* Plus, with every shipment, you'll receive the Silhouette Books Newsletter absolutely free. *And Silhouette Romance is delivered free.*

Mail the coupon today to get your four free books—and more romance than you ever bargained for.

Silhouette Romance is a service mark and a registered trademark of Simon & Schuster, Inc.

Silhouette Romance

IT'S YOUR OWN SPECIAL TIME
Contemporary romances for today's women.
Each month, six very special love stories will be yours
from SILHOUETTE.

$1.75 each

☐ 100 Stanford	☐ 127 Roberts	☐ 155 Hampson	☐ 182 Clay
☐ 101 Hardy	☐ 128 Hampson	☐ 156 Sawyer	☐ 183 Stanley
☐ 102 Hastings	☐ 129 Converse	☐ 157 Vitek	☐ 184 Hardy
☐ 103 Cork	☐ 130 Hardy	☐ 158 Reynolds	☐ 185 Hampson
☐ 104 Vitek	☐ 131 Stanford	☐ 159 Tracy	☐ 186 Howard
☐ 105 Eden	☐ 132 Wisdom	☐ 160 Hampson	☐ 187 Scott
☐ 106 Dailey	☐ 133 Rowe	☐ 161 Trent	☐ 188 Cork
☐ 107 Bright	☐ 134 Charles	☐ 162 Ashby	☐ 189 Stephens
☐ 108 Hampson	☐ 135 Logan	☐ 163 Roberts	☐ 190 Hampson
☐ 109 Vernon	☐ 136 Hampson	☐ 164 Browning	☐ 191 Browning
☐ 110 Trent	☐ 137 Hunter	☐ 165 Young	☐ 192 John
☐ 111 South	☐ 138 Wilson	☐ 166 Wisdom	☐ 193 Trent
☐ 112 Stanford	☐ 139 Vitek	☐ 167 Hunter	☐ 194 Barry
☐ 113 Browning	☐ 140 Erskine	☐ 168 Carr	☐ 195 Dailey
☐ 114 Michaels	☐ 142 Browning	☐ 169 Scott	☐ 196 Hampson
☐ 115 John	☐ 143 Roberts	☐ 170 Ripy	☐ 197 Summers
☐ 116 Lindley	☐ 144 Goforth	☐ 171 Hill	☐ 198 Hunter
☐ 117 Scott	☐ 145 Hope	☐ 172 Browning	☐ 199 Roberts
☐ 118 Dailey	☐ 146 Michaels	☐ 173 Camp	☐ 200 Lloyd
☐ 119 Hampson	☐ 147 Hampson	☐ 174 Sinclair	☐ 201 Starr
☐ 120 Carroll	☐ 148 Cork	☐ 175 Jarrett	☐ 202 Hampson
☐ 121 Langan	☐ 149 Saunders	☐ 176 Vitek	☐ 203 Browning
☐ 122 Scofield	☐ 150 Major	☐ 177 Dailey	☐ 204 Carroll
☐ 123 Sinclair	☐ 151 Hampson	☐ 178 Hampson	☐ 205 Maxam
☐ 124 Beckman	☐ 152 Halston	☐ 179 Beckman	☐ 206 Manning
☐ 125 Bright	☐ 153 Dailey	☐ 180 Roberts	☐ 207 Windham
☐ 126 St. George	☐ 154 Beckman	☐ 181 Terrill	

Silhouette Romance

IT'S YOUR OWN SPECIAL TIME
Contemporary romances for today's women.
Each month, six very special love stories will be yours
from SILHOUETTE. Look for them wherever books are sold
or order now from the coupon below.

$1.95 each

☐ 208 Halston	☐ 228 King	☐ 248 St. George	☐ 268 Hunter
☐ 209 LaDame	☐ 229 Thornton	☐ 249 Scofield	☐ 269 Smith
☐ 210 Eden	☐ 230 Stevens	☐ 250 Hampson	☐ 270 Camp
☐ 211 Walters	☐ 231 Dailey	☐ 251 Wilson	☐ 271 Allison
☐ 212 Young	☐ 232 Hampson	☐ 252 Roberts	☐ 272 Forrest
☐ 213 Dailey	☐ 233 Vernon	☐ 253 James	☐ 273 Beckman
☐ 214 Hampson	☐ 234 Smith	☐ 254 Palmer	☐ 274 Roberts
☐ 215 Roberts	☐ 235 James	☐ 255 Smith	☐ 275 Browning
☐ 216 Saunders	☐ 236 Maxam	☐ 256 Hampson	☐ 276 Vernon
☐ 217 Vitek	☐ 237 Wilson	☐ 257 Hunter	☐ 277 Wilson
☐ 218 Hunter	☐ 238 Cork	☐ 258 Ashby	☐ 278 Hunter
☐ 219 Cork	☐ 239 McKay	☐ 259 English	☐ 279 Ashby
☐ 220 Hampson	☐ 240 Hunter	☐ 260 Martin	☐ 280 Roberts
☐ 221 Browning	☐ 241 Wisdom	☐ 261 Saunders	☐ 281 Lovan
☐ 222 Carroll	☐ 242 Brooke	☐ 262 John	☐ 282 Halldorson
☐ 223 Summers	☐ 243 Saunders	☐ 263 Wilson	☐ 283 Payne
☐ 224 Langan	☐ 244 Sinclair	☐ 264 Vine	☐ 284 Young
☐ 225 St. George	☐ 245 Trent	☐ 265 Adams	☐ 285 Gray
☐ 226 Hamson	☐ 246 Carroll	☐ 266 Trent	
☐ 227 Beckman	☐ 247 Halldorson	☐ 267 Chase	

SILHOUETTE BOOKS, Department SB/1
1230 Avenue of the Americas
New York, NY 10020

Please send me the books I have checked above. I am enclosing $_____
(please add 75¢ to cover postage and handling. NYS and NYC residents please
add appropriate sales tax). Send check or money order—no cash or C.O.D.'s
please. Allow six weeks for delivery.

NAME _____

ADDRESS _____

CITY _____ STATE/ZIP _____

Let Silhouette Inspirations show you a world of Christian love and romance... for 15 days, free.

If you want to read wholesome love stories...with characters whose spiritual values are as meaningful as yours...then you'll want to read Silhouette Inspirations™ novels. You'll experience all of love's conflicts and pleasures—and the joy of happy endings—with people who share your beliefs and goals.

These books are written by Christian authors...Arlene James, Patti Beckman, Debbie Macomber, and more...for Christian readers. Each 192-page volume gives you tender romance with a message of hope and faith...and of course, a happy ending.

We think you'll be so delighted with Silhouette Inspirations, you won't want to miss a single one! We'd like to send you 2 books each month, as soon as they are published, through our Home Subscription Service. Look them over for 15 days, free. If you enjoy them as much as we think you will, pay the enclosed invoice. If not, simply return them and owe nothing.

A world of Christian love and spirituality is waiting for you...in the pages of Silhouette Inspirations novels. Return the coupon today!